THE
GIRL
ON
THE
NEWS

BOOKS BY ELISABETH CARPENTER

The Family on Smith Street

99 Red Balloons

11 Missed Calls

Only a Mother

The Woman Downstairs

The Vacancy

THE
GIRL
ON
THE
NEWS

ELISABETH
CARPENTER

bookouture

Published by Bookouture in 2024

An imprint of Storyfire Ltd.
Carmelite House
50 Victoria Embankment
London EC4Y 0DZ

www.bookouture.com

ISBN: 978-1-83790-582-9
eBook ISBN: 978-1-83790-581-2

In memory of my beautiful friend, Lou.

CHAPTER 1

Wednesday, 13th March 2024

GIRL SNATCHED WHILE VISITING GRANDMOTHER

Police and volunteers have been seen searching back gardens and sheds for four-year-old Mia Donovan.

Mia was reported missing today after being taken from Hopscotch café, close to her grandmother's home in Clayton, Manchester. Mia is described as wearing a light pink dress with large white polka dots, and white trainers. Her long, dark brown hair was in a ponytail when she was last seen at seven thirty this morning. Her mother, Jessie Donovan, 42, is distraught and appeals to whoever has taken her daughter: 'Please. If you're listening to this and you have Mia, please bring her back. I am nothing without her.'

CHAPTER 2

JESSIE

Three days earlier

I'm the designated driver on the way home from Mark's parents' house, and my shoulders relax as I turn out of their street.

'Thanks for today,' says Mark. Considering he's had two large glasses of red wine, he sounds pretty lucid. 'I really appreciate it. I know you find Mum challenging.'

'I don't mind your mum,' I say lightly, aware that I might soon get struck by lightning. 'It's nice that she invited us to her Mother's Day lunch.'

'God. Sorry, Jess. She kept going on about it being *her* day, didn't she?' He smiles wryly. 'And I'm sorry she kept going on about your studio being your *little hobby*.'

'You don't have to be sorry on her behalf. And I'll be sure to tell her about my million-pound commission, one day.'

'As long as you tell *me*, too,' he says. 'Then I can take early retirement.'

'This time next year...'

I glance in the rear-view mirror.

'Don't go to sleep yet, Mia.' I speak a little too loudly and it makes her jump. 'We'll be home soon.'

'I wasn't sleeping, Mummy,' she says, rubbing her eyes.

'I know, love. I was just making sure. You don't want to be awake till midnight with school tomorrow, do you?'

She sinks back into her car seat. At four years old, she's outgrown it – I should replace it with a booster – but she's still so little to me.

'Did you ring your mum?' Mark asks.

'Yeah, but she didn't answer. I sent her some flowers, though. I bet she's having a lie-in. She likes to celebrate everything, remember.'

'She'll probably sleep the whole day away,' he says slowly, finally showing the signs of half a bottle of merlot. 'To be honest, my ideal Father's Day would be to spend the whole day in bed.'

'Such a waste of time.'

'Exactly.' He folds his arms and sinks into the passenger seat. 'Plus, your mother's never once invited us round for Sunday lunch, so it's not as though she has a reason to get up today.'

'She lives on her own, and she's almost three hours' drive away,' I remind him, not for the first time. 'It's not the same as it is with your parents.'

He doesn't know what it's like because he was brought up in middle-class suburbia. Even though we grew up in the same town – his house was only a five-minute walk from mine – there may as well have been an ocean between us. His father retired at sixty after being in the same middle-management job for most of his life, and his mother was the *homemaker*. Those were her words, not mine. I'm not particularly sure if they like each other any more, but they muddle along.

I pull up onto our drive to find Liza sitting on the doorstep. She's reading a newspaper and has a plastic grocery bag next to her. Her short dark hair is covered with a woolly hat, and she's wearing a raincoat that looks three sizes too big for her.

'Oh, God,' says Mark. 'Why is your weird friend here on a Sunday? And why is she wearing a winter hat when it's so warm outside?'

'I invited her,' I say. 'I told you yesterday. I feel a bit sorry for her. She doesn't have many friends and her family don't have much to do with her.'

Mark groans. 'Maybe we could tell her I'm ill. Then we can spend the rest of the day together on our own as a family.' He kisses me on the cheek. 'We could watch a film together. Get the blankets out.'

'Mia would never sit through a whole film,' I say. 'But let's rain check that for next Sunday once she's gone to bed.'

'Deal.'

'You should never pretend to be ill, by the way. That's just tempting fate.' I pull up the handbrake and open the car door.

'Are you OK, Liza?' I say, getting out. 'What's happened? I thought we said three o'clock.'

She stands and stretches her legs; she's wearing jeans that are two inches above her ankles and black shoes that look like they're part of the school selection at Clarks. Strangely, she suits it. She never seems to wear the same outfit twice.

'I caught the earlier bus,' she says. 'I thought you might have been home.'

'We've been out for lunch,' I explain. 'You didn't need to wait on the step. You should've gone round the back to sit in the sun.'

'Gate's locked.'

'Oh no. Sorry, Liza.'

'You weren't to know.'

I unlock the front door while Mark helps Mia out of the car. Liza steps inside the house and heads straight to the kitchen.

She places her carrier bag on the table and takes out a bottle of pink fizz. She starts peeling off the foil.

Mark and Mia pile in with the massive amount of toys she wanted to take to lunch. His parents' house isn't exactly kid friendly.

'I had a massive row with my mum,' Liza says quietly. 'She'll never change, you know. I bought her a really nice bunch of flowers when I turned up at her house this morning with break-fast. She told me I was far too early, and she hadn't had enough warning. Even though I texted her when I set off from my flat at five this morning. It took three hours and two buses to get there. After she ate both the pastries I bought, and drank both the coffees, she went on a rant and told me exactly where I'd gone wrong in life and how I much I'd ruined hers.'

Her bottom lip starts to wobble.

Mark's eyebrows rise and his eyes dart around; he's typically uncomfortable with mere acquaintances showing this much emotion (unless it's football related). He makes a quick exit, while Mia retrieves her toy keyboard from her backpack.

'Oh dear,' I say. 'That's awful. I'm so sorry, Liza.' I put my arm around her and pull her close. 'None of those things are true, I'm sure. Maybe she was feeling under the weather?'

She sniffs, but manages to keep the tears at bay. I think she's trying to stay strong in front of Mia, who really shouldn't be listening to conversations like this.

'Hold on one second, Liza,' I say. 'I'll just sort Mia out then you'll have my full attention.' I place a handful of crackers and some cheese on a plate – Mia didn't eat much of the roast dinner at lunchtime. 'Let's go and find Daddy.'

Mia follows me into the living room, where I half-expect Mark to be horizontal on the sofa, but he's sitting on the edge of it, looking at his phone.

'That's weird,' he says. 'Three missed calls from an unknown number. Do you think they're from the same person?'

'I have no idea.'

Mia sits next to him and grabs the remote control, expertly navigating the television to *CBeebies*. I feel the familiar pang of guilt.

'Will you play a board game or something with Mia?' I ask him. 'Liza wants to talk. She's not having a good time of it, by the sound of things.'

'You're too nice to her,' he says, placing his phone next to him. 'She could be anyone. You've known her for barely a year.'

'She's harmless, Mark.'

I first met Liza when she walked into my art studio last April. It's just off the main street in town, down a cobbled path. It barely costs anything in rent because the space is tiny – a small gallery, a back room where I paint, and a bathroom with a toilet and a sink. I'd been there over two years, but she said she'd never noticed the studio before. 'Is it OK if I have a look round?' she said. The front door was open and I was working in the back room. People walk in off the street all the time, especially if it's raining. I don't get many sales from passers-by, sadly. 'Your paintings are really good,' she added. 'Did you go to art school? I've always wanted to have a go at painting. Is it difficult? Do you teach lessons?'

I chose to answer only one of those questions.

'I'm doing a one-off taster session this weekend, actually,' I said. 'Still life using acrylics on canvas. All materials supplied, plus a deli lunch.'

She signed up and paid there and then and has been popping into the studio several times a week since, often bringing me a well-needed hot chocolate, or a lemonade if it's a hot day. She takes offence if I give her the money for them, so I've started getting in some nice cookies as a way of payment in return. Not that she ever eats any.

She said it's fate that we met because we have the same

birthday. Not that I believe there's anything meaningful in coincidences.

'Have fun, you two,' I say, now, tickling the bottom of Mia's feet.

'Mummy,' she says with a little giggle as I head out the room, 'tickles are for babies.'

I almost jump when I find Liza standing in the hallway.

'Sorry,' she says. 'I wasn't creeping around or listening in. I just wondered if it was OK to use the bathroom.'

'Of course it's OK. You know where it is, right?'

She nods, then dashes up the stairs.

As I'm reaching into the fridge for the snack platter I prepared this morning, I hear the creak of a floorboard above me. Either she's using our ensuite, or she's got the wrong room. God, I hope neither Mia nor Mark have made a mess in the main bathroom. Though Mia usually tidies up after herself...

I set the plate in the middle of the kitchen table along with two white side plates and napkins. I grab two champagne flutes and place them on coasters and am rather pleased with myself with the spread. I don't usually make this much of an effort because I hardly ever have guests round. It's not just Liza who has a pitiful amount of friends, but I don't mind. I have my painting, Mia, Mark. And I'm busy enough in my head.

'This looks amazing!'

Liza makes me jump for the second time.

I really must try to be more *present*.

'Thank you!' I say, taking glory where I can. As an artist, I'm used to people being a bit *too* honest about my work. At least with a snack platter, it's not so personal.

Liza sits and pours the wine she opened into the two tall glasses. She takes a long sip.

'God, I needed that after the day I've had,' she says. 'I hate Mother's Day.'

I'm not sure I know her well enough to ask her if she's experienced a heartbreaking loss that makes her feel this way – it would be cruel to ask. She's the kind of person who'd feel obliged to answer honestly.

'I'm sorry to hear that,' I say, instead.

'Thank God I don't have kids of my own. That'd just add to the disappointment of it all.'

'Oh.'

'People always expect women in their forties to have children or to want to have children, but it's just not my thing. Apart from Mia, they're all nightmares.'

'You were a kid once,' I say.

'Exactly. Plus, I can't guarantee I wouldn't turn into my mother.'

'Has your mum always been like that to you?'

She shrugs. 'I guess. I've nothing to compare it to, really. I didn't see much of my grandparents or aunties and uncles when I was growing up. We moved away from our hometown after... She got a new job somewhere else. Isolated herself, really.'

She tops up her glass, then drinks the whole thing. She fills it up again.

'Careful, Liza. It's only quarter past three – you'll be on the floor in no time if you carry on like that. I've never seen you drink so quickly.'

'Sorry.' She pushes the glass away. 'Sorry, Jess. I don't want to spoil your day.'

'It's not *my* day. I didn't mean to be your drink monitor. I just want to make sure you're OK.' I rip off a chunk of bread and lay a piece of cheese on top. 'Here, eat this. It'll soak it up. And I've made up the spare room in case you need it.'

'Have you really?' Her eyes brim with unshed tears. 'You're a star, Jess. I don't know what I'd do without you. I've never had a friend who would do that for me.' She takes a bite of the bread and chews and swallows loudly. She leans back in her chair and looks around the kitchen. 'You really do have the perfect life, don't you, Jess? Perfect house, perfect business, perfect husband, perfect daughter.'

'It didn't come easy.'

'Really?' She tilts her head to the side. 'I suppose you could lose it just like that.' She snaps her fingers. 'You never know.' She places her hand over mine. 'I'd be here for you,' she says. 'If you lost everything. You're like a sister to me.'

'I...' I don't know what to say, this is all quite bleak.

She shakes her head slightly.

'Anyway. Enough of all this depressing talk,' she says, pulling the glass towards her again. 'Are you painting anything interesting at the moment? One day, you could paint me. Though I'd have to wait till I've saved enough money. Your paintings are pretty expensive.'

'I barely cover minimum wage once I've added up all the hours it takes,' I say. 'But it's worth it. I can't imagine doing anything else.'

'One day I'll have a job I love,' she says.

'You'll find somewhere. Didn't you say you had an interview next week?'

'Yeah,' she says. 'It's tomorrow. Ten in the morning. But it'll be the same as everywhere else. It must be me. I'm the problem.'

'We can practise today,' I offer. I take a large sip of wine – I need to catch up a little. 'You need to be more positive. Then good things will come to you.'

Even though she's the same age as I am, she looks and acts so much younger. I feel as protective over her – in this moment – as Mark does with me all the time. It's like she needs someone to look after her, but at the same time she's so fiercely resilient. If I wasn't here for her, I suspect she'd soon find someone else to replace me.

Perhaps I've had a sip too many, too.

'Yes,' she says, thinking. 'I'll try to be more like you. Do you think you can teach me?'

* * *

Mia's squeaky clean after her bath and looking adorable in the tiger-stripe onesie that Mark laid out for her. He stands at the kitchen door as Mia comes over to kiss me goodnight.

'Hang on a sec,' he says, holding up his phone. 'It's that number again. I'll answer it this time and see what they want. They've called another seven times since we got back this afternoon.'

'Oh dear,' Liza says to me. 'I hope it's nothing sinister. What if someone's cloned his identity and stolen all his money? Or what if he's having an affair and it's the other person's spouse wanting to speak to him?'

My mouth drops open slightly.

She's drunk most of the bottle of pink prosecco and has started the new one. I think I've had a glass and a half judging by my aching head.

'Sorry, sorry,' she says. 'I have an overactive imagination. It comes with living alone. I've made up backstories for all the people living on my street. Drug dealers, people in Witness Protection, a woman who killed her husband and sealed his body in the pantry wall.' She clocks my face again. 'It's not real. I'm not weird, I promise. I guess the truth is far more mundane.'

'If we could keep it PG in front of Mia, so we don't give her nightmares,' I say, though Mia doesn't scare easily. Except for the tooth fairy – she was relieved to learn it doesn't actually exist. I pour some milk into her plastic cup and blast it for ten in the microwave. 'Daddy won't be long, Mia.'

I place the milk on her little drawing table, and she pulls up her chair. She sits, patiently, with her hands under her swinging legs.

Mark's still on the phone – I can't hear what he's saying in the hall and he has his back to me. When he turns round, he's frowning. He strides across the kitchen and opens the patio door. It feels as though the whole house shakes when he slams it shut.

Liza's patting her lap. 'Come and say goodnight to me, Mia.'

Mia's blowing on her cup of warm milk, oblivious.

'See,' says Liza. 'Children can sense it with me. They hate me.'

'Mia doesn't hate you,' I say quietly. 'She's just concentrating.'

'I told you, Jess. I hate Mother's Day. And Mother's Day hates me.'

'I won't be a minute,' I say. 'Have some more bread while I take Mia up. We can order a pizza, if you like.'

I take Mia's hand and her mug, and we walk down the hall then slowly up the stairs.

'Why's Liza talking funny?' she asks.

'She's tired, that's all.'

'Why doesn't she go to sleep, then?'

'Because she doesn't want to be rude, I guess. She's going to be sleeping in the spare room tonight.'

'OK, Mummy.' We finally reach the top of the stairs. 'Can I have a sleepover with one of my friends next week?'

'Course you can.'

In her bedroom, I place her cup on her bedside cabinet. She pulls back her covers and crawls into bed.

'Will Daddy come and say goodnight?'

'He will when he's finished on the phone.'

'He's been watching his phone for hours. Is Daddy OK? He didn't talk much today.'

'*He's* tired, too.'

'I'm tired,' she says, lying her head on the pillow. 'You're the only one not tired. You've got to look after us all.'

I smile, stroking her soft round cheek.

'I will. Don't worry.' I kiss the top of her head. 'I'll leave the landing light on until you fall asleep.'

'Thank you, Mummy.'

I leave the door ajar before going back downstairs.

In the kitchen, Liza's standing at the patio door, looking out at the darkness of our back garden.

'Everything OK?'

Liza doesn't flinch; she's less jumpy than I am.

'I didn't know Mark smoked,' she says.

'Not for years,' I say, standing next to her.

'He was shouting at whoever he's talking to.'

'Really? What about?'

'I don't know. I couldn't hear the details.' She turns to face me. 'Can I go to bed now? I've had too much to drink and I feel a bit funny.'

I glance at the digital display on the oven. It's only eight o'clock. I had a feeling this might happen.

Maybe Mark and I will have the chance to watch a film together after all.

She walks towards the hallway. 'Is it the second on the left upstairs?'

'Yep. And I've left a towel and some pyjamas on the bed.' I grab a bottle of water from the fridge. 'Take this, too. You might need it in the night.'

'Thank you, Jess.' She smiles. 'You really think of every-thing, don't you?'

'I try.'

'You should have a break,' she says. 'You do too much for other people. Somewhere nice on your own. By the seaside. Artists like solitude, don't they?'

'It depends.'

'Anyway. Night night. Thanks again.'

'Night.'

I watch as she walks up the stairs – her eyes fixed ahead.

Mark's right. I don't know her well at all. It's become evident after seeing her behaviour tonight. One minute she was so sweet, calling me the best friend she's ever had; the next a shadow appeared in her eyes, and she said whatever came to mind.

I suppose her drinking on an empty stomach is what caused it. I hope I don't come to regret letting her stay tonight. But what's the worst that could happen?

CHAPTER 3
SADIE

15th January 1995

Sadie Harrison – Junior Reporter, *Preston Times*

Interview with Rosemarie (Rosie) McShane (DoB: 29/01/1982)

Notes:

Before my interview with Rosie, and in order to give context to the case, I have examined police interviews, and notes from the child psychologist [name redacted] whose notes included 'She doesn't seem sorry' and 'Rosie isn't accepting any responsibility at all'.

This extract is from the first police interview of Rosie McShane (RM), conducted by Detective Inspector Graham Paterson (DI), and later joined by Police Constable Angela McVey (AM).

Police Interview date: 14th March 1994

Rosie McShane's age at initial interview: Twelve years, one month, and fifteen days.

(…) Denotes indistinguishable words or a long pause.

The following excerpt was played in court.

RM: But I don't want my dad to be here. Or my mum. Can someone else be with me instead? That lady who sat next to me in the car on the way here. What's her name? I think she said it was Angela but I didn't hear her properly.

DI: We haven't managed to get hold of your mother yet, but some-one's gone to collect your dad from your house.

RM: Can you cancel it? He'll be really cross. You should see him when my brother Billy makes him angry.

DI: I'll see what I can do.

RM: He'll tell you to let me go. He's not a big fan of the police, you know.

DI: That wasn't the impression I got from him. He was very co-opera-tive when we talked to him yesterday.

RM: He wouldn't *tell* you he didn't like you. You'd probably arrest him. But if he finds out you've taken me here, he'll kick off.

DI Graham Paterson leaves the room and re-enters after three minutes, twenty seconds. WPC Angela McVey enters the interview room.

RM: Can you sit next to me, Angela? Is that your name?

AM: Yes, all right.

DI: We're going to talk about what happened yesterday, Rosie. Do you remember what happened?

RM: Mostly.

DI: On the afternoon of Sunday, the thirteenth of March, you said you were out playing with your next door neighbour, Lauren Jones. Is that right?

RM: I told that to the other man, the other policeman. Didn't he tell you?

DI: He wrote it down, Rosie, when he talked to you at your Auntie Maureen's house. Will you tell me about what happened when you were with Lauren who lives next door?

RM: Maureen's not really my auntie, she lives next door to us on the other side. My mum told me to call all her friends aunties, but I'm too old for that now. And Lauren's not just my neighbour, she's my best friend. She's like my sister. We've known each other since we were in Infants.

DI: Since you both started at Priory Lane Primary?

RM: We used to walk there together. Every day. Because it's only down the road, about twenty minutes, I think. We used to hold hands when we first started because we were only four, and her mum would wave to us from her doorstep. It was well cute. She's really nice is Laurie's mum. We get the bus now we're at the high school.

DI: Let's go back to yesterday—

RM: I knocked for Laurie at half past nine. It's the same time every day at the weekend because that's when Davy – I mean 'Dad' – wakes up for his job. He works at the cash and carry that's open every day. Anyway, Lauren had 50p and she said she'd share it with me, and we went to the corner shop, the one that Mrs Tony works at. Her name's Mrs Alderton really, but it's too hard for the little kids to say. But it was shut because it was Sunday yesterday. I wish she'd open on Sundays because Davy says they're allowed to now. The pub sells sweets in the little shop on the side of it, but that doesn't open till eleven.

DI: And what happened during the rest of the afternoon? Did you go back home for your lunch?

RM: I went back to Laurie's and her mum left us out some bread and jam and butter. They had marmite, too, but I'm not a big fan.

DI: Did you stay there long?

RM: No. Her mum was watching something on the telly and she kept telling us to shh and be quiet. Laurie had picked her some daffodils from the field and we put them in a Tupperware beaker – or it might've been a pint glass, I can't remember. We filled it with water. Lauren's mum liked them, but she didn't like us being loud, talking about Shane from school. Lauren likes him but I do as well. Anyway, Lauren's mum said we had to give her some *bloody peace* and to *get some fresh air*.

DI: Did you get *your* mum any flowers?

RM: Yeah – half of the ones we picked. I put them in an empty milk bottle – I washed it out first. I don't know if she liked them or not cos I didn't see her. Billy probably said they were from him. I should've written a message to go with them.

(…)

DI: Where was your mum?

RM: I dunno. She might've been in bed because she was up late on Saturday night.

DI: Did you and Lauren argue about Shane?

RM: Huh? Why would we argue about Shane? He doesn't know who we are. Just like Ross Bradshaw didn't.

DI: You said you both liked him.

RM: We do. But that happens all the time. We always like the same boys. It's not as though they ask us out.

DI: So what happened after that?

RM: We called on Samantha who was at her gran's house because she visits sometimes at weekends and school holidays. Then we went to the park in the forest. It's just a bit of grass now. There's not much to do around here. There used to be some wooden benches and a table, but the older ones wrecked them.

DI: This is the Samantha you said you were with in the afternoon?

RM: Yes, we all played hide and seek. I didn't really want to play it because it's so babyish, so I went into the den to chill out. Lauren said she was going to go home because she doesn't like Sam that much.

DI: Don't you and Lauren usually stick together?

RM: Mostly. But I didn't want to upset Sam because we don't see her much and she doesn't know anyone else round here.

DI: How did Lauren end up in the field?

RM: She uses it as a short cut. She probably needed a rest – she always gets tired easily.

DI: Can you remember what happened just before Lauren's mother came out?

RM: I found her lying on the ground. She had flowers in her hair, which was weird because she's never put them in her hair like that before. Fast asleep, she was.

DI: Lauren wasn't asleep, though, was she?

RM: I don't know. I thought she was. I've not seen her since her mum carried her away.

DI: She died, didn't she, Rosie?

RM: I don't know. I didn't see it happen. She was like that when I found her.

DI: You said you two did everything together. You were best friends. You lied about playing hide and seek, didn't you?

RM: I said we *mostly* sticked together. I don't know what happened to her. I really don't.

DI: Then where were you when Lauren was harmed?

RM: I was with Samantha, I told you. After she found me in the den. She was crying so I helped her back to her gran's. You have to believe me. I don't lie.

DI: Samantha's grandmother said she didn't see you.

RM: I don't think her gran saw me. I waited at the end of their path by the gate so I knew she'd got in safe. Sam went straight inside then she shut the front door. Ask Sam. She'll tell you.

DI: Lauren's mother said she saw you leaning over Lauren. You were the only one there. Who else could've hurt her? Were you even with Samantha that afternoon?

RM: I was asking Lauren to wake up. I wanted Laurie to wake up.

DI: You know exactly what happened to her, don't you? Lauren's mother said you were just sitting there. You weren't asking Lauren to wake up because you knew she *wouldn't* wake up. Just tell the truth, Rosie. You need to tell us what happened to her.

(…)

RM: No, no, no.

(…)

AM: Calm down, Rosie. Here, have a tissue.

RM: I don't know what happened to her. I really don't (…) I want my mum.

AM: It's going to be OK, Rosie.

(...)

RM: I want my mum.

CHAPTER 4

HEATHER

It been thirty years since I lost my Lauren. My only child; the light and joy of my life.

Though, I didn't lose her.

She was taken from me.

Murdered by her best friend.

When I close my eyes, I'm there in that moment. I can see it so clearly, so vividly.

It was a Sunday, the thirteenth of March 1994. Mother's Day, like today.

I heard the scream through the kitchen window that was only slightly open. I was still wearing my apron when I bolted out the front door.

Marie from the house next door was sitting on her doorstep, smoking.

'Did you hear that?' I said to her. I was wearing my slippers and the pavement was chilling my feet. 'It was so loud.'

Marie took a long drag of her cigarette and shrugged.

'It sounded like Lauren,' I pressed. 'Did you hear the screaming?'

She exhaled.

'Marie!' I wanted to shake her by the shoulders; she was probably hungover – in another world. 'Have you seen the girls?'

Her son Billy opened their front door. He was wearing shorts and a black T-shirt.

'What's going on?' he said.

'There's always screaming and shrieking around here,' said Marie, leaning against the doorframe. 'We're on an estate with about a hundred kids. I don't know why you're so worried. Lauren and Rosie are well past the age for screaming.'

I started to run.

I didn't know why I was so worried, either. Because she was right: kids shouted and screeched all the time.

But I hadn't seen Lauren for hours.

I was running faster than I had done in years. Past the sweet shop, towards a group of boys kicking a football in the road.

They stopped when they saw me. You didn't get many mothers who jogged, let alone run, in this area.

'Have you seen Lauren?' I asked them.

One of them – I think it was the Davidson kid from number seventy-eight – pointed to the field that was hidden by trees and shrubs.

I pushed through the gap created by people much smaller than me.

'Laurie,' I shouted. 'Are you here, love?'

I saw them forty feet away. I started to run again.

Lauren was lying on her back; Rosie was leaning over her.

'Laurie?' Thirty feet away. 'Didn't you hear me calling?'

Lauren didn't move. Rosie didn't look up.

I slowed down when I was almost near her. It was like I knew something was very wrong.

Her eyes were closed. Daisies and buttercups decorated the hair around her face. Her arms were wide open, like she was waiting for a hug.

I collapsed beside her; shook her gently by the shoulders.

'Laurie, love. Wake up.' She wasn't breathing. 'Please, Laurie. Please wake up.'

I scooped her into my arms; the adrenaline made it effortless.

'What did you do to her, Rosie?' I screamed at the silent child.

My knees buckled slightly as I stood.

I needed to get help. I needed her to wake up. I needed to call an ambulance.

I hesitated for only a second, but Rosie didn't say a word.

I open my eyes, now, to escape what happened next.

When I scooped her into my arms that horrific day, I wanted everything to cease. I wanted the world to stop turning; for time to freeze and rewind to the minute she was alive and I could stop her from dying.

But everything kept going. People went about their lives. Her school friends left school – left town, settled down. Had families of their own.

Thirty years ago. A long time, yet a blink of an eye.

She'd be forty-two now. A mother herself perhaps.

I only have two photos of her displayed. One in the dining room, and the other on my nightstand where I can say good morning and goodnight. Anything more is too painful. I used to have photographs of her scattered around the house, but seeing her face when I didn't expect to sends me back to that awful time and place. I don't know when it will get better. Sometimes, it's like she's still here, watching over me. Telling me in my dreams that there's something I don't know.

My husband Eddie is hovering at the living-room window.

'I can't see why you can't drive yourself,' he says, his key ring looped through his fingers. 'The more times you get behind the wheel, the easier it'll get. And it's not as if you've crashed it – I don't know why you're so scared.'

'Just for today, Eddie,' I say, taking my black blazer off its hanger on the back of the living-room door. He's stopped questioning why I wear black on Mother's Day. 'I wouldn't be able to concentrate. It's not fair on others on the road. And don't jinx things by saying I haven't had an accident yet. That's sure to tempt fate.'

'OK, OK,' he says, holding up his palms – calming me down as though I've been ranting. It's totally over the top and he knows it grates on me. He drops his hands after I tilt my head and raise my eyebrows in the way that grates on *him*. 'Can I—?'

'Yes, you can wait in the car.'

He'd only sulk if I made him sit with me. Eddie's usually good in company, but he runs out of things to talk about with my mother. Especially in *that place*.

'I don't know how she can bear it in there,' he says, as though reading my mind. 'Doing the same things week in, week out. Bingo today, isn't it? Hosted by that pair of idiots they give a microphone to.'

'I've put your name on the waiting list for a room,' I say as I smooth my hair in front of the hall mirror. 'Seeing as you like it so much.'

He kisses me on the cheek.

'Very funny.' He opens the front door. 'You'd miss me like mad, you know you would.'

'I suppose.'

We head out the door, towards the car, and the sunlight hurts my eyes a little. As usual, he opens the passenger door for me, waits till I'm in and closes it gently. He does his little jog round to the driver's side and gets in.

'The Haven' – he starts the ignition – 'here we come. I can't contain my excitement.'

I tap him on his thigh.

'Give over, Eddie.'

I look out the window to hide my smile.

If it weren't for Eddie, I don't think I'd still be here.

* * *

It's not as bad as he makes it out to be. It's a modern two-storey building with lots of windows and huge potted plants scattered along the path that runs across the front. Sliding doors open as I give Eddie a little wave. He's as happy as anything, with his newspaper and a coffee from Costa. Who knew you could buy happiness for just £4.95?

'Good morning, Heather.' It's Paddy on reception today. I love Paddy. 'If I could just take your autograph.' He hands me a pen for the Visitors' Book. 'Lovely day outside today,' he says as I write. 'Glad we have big windows in this place or I'd never see daylight.'

'Are you chained to that desk again, Paddy?'

I place the pen in the crease of the book.

'Twelve-hour shift,' he says, sitting on his wheelie chair. He spins around. 'But you know me. Always have a smile. Because if you can't smile...?'

'Then, what's the point?'

'You read my mind, Heather.'

It helps that he says exactly the same things every time I visit.

'Give Patricia my best,' he shouts as I walk along the corridor.

Room twelve – the same number as the house we lived in when my sister and I were kids. It was the time my dad used to work away more than he was at home. My mother hates that she's in room twelve, which is why there's a yellow Post-it note with the words *Pat's Office* covering it.

'Happy Mother's Day,' I say as I walk in. I place the cluster of carnations on the small coffee table in the little seating area. 'Where's that vase you usually keep on your bedside cabinet?'

She's sitting with a tartan blanket on her lap even though it's boiling hot in here.

'It's ridiculous,' she says, looking out the window into the courtyard outside, 'saying that at your age.'

'Saying what?'

'Happy Mother's Day.'

I bend to kiss her on the cheek and sit on the padded stool in front of her.

'Why is that ridiculous? You're still my mother. You'd go mad if I didn't say it, wouldn't you?'

She turns to face me, a hint of mischief in her eyes. She's been so contrary these past few weeks and I'm still trying to understand her changing personalities. One day, she's the mother I remember as a child; sometimes, she's how she was as a grandmother to Lauren. Strict, then as carefree as a bird on a breeze.

'You're not wrong.' She peers over her glasses at the carrier bag I brought with me. 'What else have you got there?'

I reach in.

'A box of chocolates' – I place it on her lap, trying not to laugh – 'a novel by that *woman writer* you like' – I place that on her lap, too – 'a bag of Werther's Original... and three magazines.'

She wraps her arms around her loot.

'You're such a funny one,' she says. 'Oh, I do love presents.'

'I know you do, Mum.'

I stand and try to flatten a bit of hair that's sticking up at the back of her head.

'They never do it right for me, love,' she says. 'Will you brush it for me? It's in the drawer on the left.'

'Of course, Mum.' The soft-bristled brush is one of those old-fashioned ones that has embroidered material on the back. I gently smooth it from the crown of her head to the nape of her neck. 'That's not too hard, is it?'

'It's just right.'

We're silent for a few moments. I'm trying to take everything in – trying to capture every snapshot of being with her because I know we won't have long.

These moments of role reversal have been creeping up on us. When she still lived in her own terraced house around the corner, I cooked her dinner and ran a couple of errands. A few years later, I was going round three times a day to prepare her meals and to check she was taking her cholesterol medication. Just before Christmas it had got to the stage where if she was alone, she wouldn't eat, wash, go outside, or pick up the telephone. I didn't mind being there for her, but I couldn't sleep for worrying. It was then that my sister and I decided she'd be safer in here.

'It's a good job I was nice to you when you were a child,' she says. Everyone's a mind-reader today. 'If I wasn't, I doubt you'd be doing this for me now. Though, saying that, your sister hasn't been in to see me today. I doubt she'd brush my hair.'

'She'll be busy,' I reply, placing the brush down and sitting back on the stool. 'She's always busy, you know that.'

'I don't know that,' says Mum. 'She *makes* herself busy. What's the use in that?'

The undertone is that my sister never had children – has never wanted children. And now at the grand old age of fifty-seven, she's well past being too late.

'I think about her a lot,' Mum adds. She's talking about Lauren, now. She reaches over and takes my hand. 'Especially now I'm in here. There's too much time to think now I don't have to do my own washing, my own cleaning. I'll look after her, you know. When I get there... when I'm...'

'I don't want to think about that, Mum. You're not going anywhere.'

'We both know that's not true.' She looks out the window

again, at three noisy children hurling pulled-off tree blossom at each other. 'She's been coming to me when I'm not asleep.'

'What?'

My heart gives a jolt.

They say that when people are close to dying, they start seeing relatives and friends – those who have passed before them. I've never truly believed that. It's a trick the brain plays on us so we're not fearful of the inevitable.

I've visited countless mediums and psychics over the years. They put the fear into me that my little girl is out there, lost – her spirit wandering the earth because of the cruel way she was taken from us. But I have found no evidence that any one of those charlatans were actually talking to my daughter. They should be ashamed of themselves, preying on the heartbroken like that.

'What did she say to you?' I ask.

'She didn't say anything,' Mum replies. 'I'd have rung you straight away if she'd spoken. No...' Mum takes off her tartan blanket and flings it onto her bed. 'She just sits on the end of the bed with her legs crossed like she used to do in school assemblies. I wish she'd spoken, so I could give you a message.'

'Me, too, Mum.'

'It's hard for you on days like these, isn't it?'

I nod, my lips pressed together to stop myself from bursting into tears.

'It's hard for you every day, no doubt.' She reaches over for the box of chocolates, takes out my favourite – the orange cream – and places it on my lap. 'If I could, I'd take the pain from you. Just like Lauren was to you, you're *my* little girl. My heart breaks for you, Heather.'

I stand, reach over for a tissue, and wipe the tears while facing the window.

The kids outside have found a hosepipe and are shrieking and screaming, getting themselves soaking wet.

I sit back down and open my chocolate.

'Jesus,' says Mum, opening one for herself, 'I wish they'd keep it down. Noisy little shits.'

She gives me a wink before popping the chocolate into her mouth.

CHAPTER 5

SADIE

15th January 1995

Sadie Harrison – Junior Reporter, *Preston Times*

Interview with Rosemarie (Rosie) McShane aged 12 years, eleven months.

Length of time imprisoned to date: Two months.

Location: A small room in Castleton Secure Unit, Merseyside – a facility for young offenders (both male and female) aged between twelve and sixteen years of age.

Notes:

Castleton is located in-between a residential area and an industrial estate and is surrounded by trees and shrubs. I was greeted by the manager, Elaine Bushell, who was keen to show me the measures she has implemented in the attempt to revamp and modernise the rehabilitation of young people. She mentioned that I was not the first journalist who has requested to talk to Rosie, but didn't elaborate who when I asked.

I was led past four classrooms, which were all quite noisy. Each boy and girl was paired with an adult. In one of the classrooms, they were discussing the harmful effects of cocaine and ecstasy.

We walked through a lounge area with bright yellow walls and three huge settees. I caught sight of the games room that housed two pool tables, various board games, and, surprisingly, a dart board.

'They're only allowed access to that room if they've had three blue cards in a row,' said Elaine.

She explained that the young people – she doesn't refer to them as inmates – are given blue cards for good behaviour and yellow cards for swearing and bad behaviour. Three yellow cards, or a physical assault, will result in a red card. Red cards involve their behaviour being logged in their files.

When I inquired about the percentage of children here reoffending, Elaine explained this was high. 'For most of the young people,' she said, 'this is their fifth or sixth time here. And of course, after the age of sixteen, they're sent to Young Offender's Institutions, which are more like adult prisons.'

Rosie McShane is sitting at a table in an open-plan area, adjacent to a television room, and two large corridors. It has several bookcases and framed photographs (red telephones boxes and London buses).

This is the first time I have seen her since the trial, but she has never met me.

Elaine introduces us before entering her office, which is only a few metres away.

Rosie doesn't stand to greet me, though I didn't expect her to. Her hair is in a short bob and she's wearing a black polo neck jumper, and large gold hoop earrings. Her eyes are framed with thick brown eyeliner; her lips coated with clear lip gloss. She looks several years older than she did just a few months ago.

Time: 09:45

Sadie Harrison (SH): Rosie, I'm Sadie Harrison. Thanks for letting me visit.

Rosie McShane (RM): I've never met a reporter before. Elaine says loads have asked to see me. One of them wanted to make a documentary, but what's the point if you can't see our faces? Are you on the telly as well?

SH: No. I work for the local paper. How are you finding it in here?

RM: It's always this noisy. Even at night-time. Kids press their buzzers just for a laugh because we're locked in at night. I wish I were back at home.

SH: Are you sleeping OK?

RM: I guess. Sometimes, in the middle of the night, you can feel them watching you, and when I open my eyes, there she is – the night lady – peeking through the window. They're always watching us in here. Look, there are cameras everywhere.

SH: I suppose it's to keep you safe.

RM: Yeah, from everyone else. They can be right nasty in here.

(…)

RM: What are you going to say about me in your article?

SH: It's a piece about children who (…) find themselves in circumstances such as yours.

RM: You mean locked up when they didn't do it?

SH: I...

RM: Because I didn't. My keyworker says it's better if I just accept it and say I'm sorry. But how can I be sorry for something that I didn't do? She said it might be because I'm blocking it out – that my brain is protecting me from the horrible thing I did.

SH: Do you think she's right?

RM: No. How could I block out hurting Lauren? It doesn't make sense. I know what I did, and what I didn't do. (…) I really miss her.

(…)

SH: Is it all right if I ask you some questions about your home life – before you came here?

RM: OK.

SH: Can you describe your house?

RM: I talked about it in court. And they played my interviews for everyone to hear. Do I have to do it again?

SH: I want to know how you feel about it now – when you're not under so much pressure.

RM: It'll be no different.

SH: Would you rather talk about something else?

RM: Probably not. Everything's a bit shit, isn't it?

*(**Note:** Rosie's eyes flashed, wanting a reaction from me. In previous interviews I've read she has not used any swear words. This, possibly, is due to her current surroundings.)*

RM: OK, then. I lived with my mum and my uncle Davy even though I was meant to call him 'dad'. He's not my real uncle and he's not my real dad, either. He moved in because my mum worked a lot – at first he was her boyfriend, but I think they ended up just friends. She worked at night, mainly at the pub on the corner. Sometimes she cleaned people's houses. The posh people on the other estate.

SH: Did anyone else live with you?

RM: My brother, and we had a cat and a dog. We didn't see the cat much. I think it went to the lady who lived across the road because she was always feeding her. She probably wanted to steal her cos her cat was run over. Tilly was our dog. I think she's still alive. (…) Do you know what one of the policemen described my house like? In front of everyone in the court?

SH: Go on.

RM: They said it was like a shell.

SH: What do you think about that?

RM: I think they meant we didn't have much stuff, so it might be that. No photos or anything. No books like they have in here. Lauren's house was full of ornaments and bookcases. Stuff everywhere.

SH: Do you think they meant it in an emotional way?

RM: No. The police are interested in facts more than feelings, aren't they? They like the truth, or what they think is the truth.

SH: What do you think makes a home?

RM: I dunno. This place is more like a home than my house – more noise, more talking – though I shouldn't really say that because my brother and my mum still live there. Well, I think they do. Mum said that Davy left. Some of the older ones in here have a telly in their own room, did you know that?

SH: That's nice.

RM: I guess. You know, they just let us kids do what we wanted back home. They didn't care where we were until it was getting dark. Just before the summer holidays, I saw a woman slap little Bradley Wooton round the head in the street because he was playing near an open drain. And no one cared, you know, that she was hitting him. He wasn't doing anything naughty; he was almost a metre away from the hole. And Bradley isn't even her kid. She said to him, 'Tell your mum I've given you a thrashing so she doesn't have to.' As if his mum would believe that.

SH: Believe what?

RM: That he'd already been punished.

SH: Do you miss being at home?

RM: Yes. I miss Tilly. Do you think they'll let her visit?

SH: I'm not sure (…) I read through your police interview, Rosie. You mentioned flowers in Lauren's hair. Do you know how they got there?

RM: No.

SH: Did you ever make daisy chains?

RM: Sometimes, when I was younger. Lauren and me just liked to chat, you know. Mainly about boys and how we were going to be more confident and stuff. But when we hung round with Samantha – which wasn't often, really – we played silly games because Sam's a year younger than us and she has brothers so she always wanted to play football or hide and seek, or climb trees.

SH: So you were definitely playing with Sam that day?

RM: Why would I lie about something like that? It's not *my* fault they got the wrong person. And now I'm stuck in here and everyone's forgotten about me.

SH: I'm sorry you feel like that, Rosie.

RM: The police didn't try hard enough to talk to Sam because they thought she was lying for me. At Christmas she was caught stealing Mars bars from the garage shop, so they just thought she was a liar *and* a thief, but she wasn't at all.

SH: Even though she was caught stealing?

RM: It wasn't Sam who pinched the chocolate. (…) Just because Lauren's mum found me with Lauren, doesn't mean I hurt her. But it doesn't matter now, does it? They – people who don't even know me – thought I did it. They found me guilty.

SH: It does matter.

RM: My solicitor will tell you. Have you managed to talk to her? She believed me.

SH: She did?

RM: Do you think she was lying?

SH: No, I—

RM: I don't want to talk about it any more.

SH: I'll make an appointment to see her. I promise.

RM: Right...

SH: What?

RM: I thought you'd have talked to her already. Never mind.

SH: I will.

RM: So, how many other kids in here do you talk to?

SH: No one else.

RM: I like that. We have to share everything in here – except our beds, thank God. Do you have kids?

SH: No.

RM: Do you get bored? I can come and visit you when I'm finished if you like. I don't think it'll be long now. I've been here for *ages*.

SH: Have they told you how long you'll be in here for?

RM: I didn't ask.

CHAPTER 6

HEATHER

'You left your phone in the car,' Eddie says when I open the door. 'Your sister's rung three times.'

'Didn't you answer it?'

'I did when she rang for the third time, otherwise there'd have been a fourth, a fifth and a sixth.'

'What did she want?' I get in and close the door.

'To speak to you.'

He starts the car and reverses out the parking space.

'Obviously,' I say. 'Did she give you a hint about the subject?'

Sometimes it's like pulling teeth trying to get information out of him.

'I didn't ask,' he says. 'It's not as though it's an unusual occurrence. She rings you about three times a day. No doubt she'll bombard you with one of her stories.'

He opens the glove compartment and takes out my phone, placing it on my lap.

'What did you put it in there for?'

'A bit of peace and quiet, that's what for.'

'You're a funny one, Eddie.'

My sister's face appears on my screen as the phone rings.

'Heather,' she says. 'At last!'

'Have you been running? What's the panic?'

'Just ringing to see how you are.'

'I've just been in to see Mum.' I glance at my husband, who's pretending not to listen. 'Did Eddie not tell you?'

'No, he just said you were unavailable.'

I roll my eyes.

'Aren't you going to see Mum today?' I ask her. 'It's Mother's Day.'

'I know what day it is.' She sounds as though she's in a railway station. 'Hopefully I can be there by the end of the day.'

'What's so urgent?'

'I've found you another group.'

'What sort of group?'

'A bereavement group. I've heard really good things about it.'

'I've tried loads of those talking therapy places. They're not for me. They didn't help at all.'

'This one's different,' she says. 'Please, Heather. For me.'

There's four years between us – I'm the eldest, obviously. When she was born, our mother said I'd tell everyone she was *my* baby. I doted on her, helped bath her, picked out her clothes, refilled her juice cup. My unconditional love and attention lasted until she was about thirteen and became extremely difficult and spoiled. I fear this was of my doing. She's not like that now, though. Obviously.

'There's a meeting tomorrow morning at ten,' she goes on. 'I could drive you there and we can get a nice breakfast before it starts. I'll pick somewhere that does hash browns. And proper coffee.'

I sigh dramatically. 'OK, I'll do it for you.'

It must be that I'm hungry right now to have agreed to it.

By the time we say our goodbyes, Eddie and I are pulling

into the cemetery car park.

We get out the car and he opens the boot. I pick up the flower arrangement I spent most of yesterday working on: daffodils, yellow carnations, tiny roses, and a scattering of baby's breath.

The plastic brightly coloured windmills that are placed next to a couple of gravestones in the children's area always make me smile – as does the tinkling windchimes that sound in the gentle breeze.

There's a woman kneeling in front of the grave three ones along from Lauren's. She looks about the same age as me, but she's been carrying her sadness for two years longer than I have. We exchange good afternoons and leave each other alone. Always the same. I don't know even her name. One day I'll ask.

Eddie bends down to pick a few weeds from the gravel that have managed to pop up since last week.

'There you go, love,' he says to her, pocketing the green leaves.

'I've just been to see your granny,' I say, placing the flowers. 'She's getting worse and she knows it. She said she saw you, Laurie. I hope it was really you, but I know…'

I feel a drop of rain on my cheek, and a little silver helium heart balloon taps on her stone. Some people might take it as a sign; I wish I were one of them.

'I saw Jamie Sanderson yesterday,' I tell her. 'He and his wife are expecting their second child. Can you believe it – little Jamie Sanderson? He's as tall as me now. He recognised me faster than I did him. He said he often thinks of you. That's nice of him, isn't it? Lots of people think about you, Laurie. You'll never be forgotten.'

The rain comes down harder now; thick, grey clouds are gathering. The heart-shaped balloon untethers and floats into the sky.

It's a good job I don't believe in signs.

CHAPTER 7

13th March 2024

Is Missing Girl the Victim of a Child Murderer?
By Jonathan Ainsworth for the *Manchester Post*

Fears have been raised that missing four-year-old Mia Donovan could be a victim of a serial killer.

The shock claim comes thirty years after Rosie McShane – herself only twelve years old at the time – was jailed for seven years for killing her best friend Lauren Jones. It was a crime that shook the country. McShane was released in 2002 after spending almost seven years behind bars and was given a whole new identity. Heather Jones, Lauren's mother, said at the time of Rosie McShane's release: 'We always believed McShane was a cold and calculated killer, and who's to say she hasn't changed? There's no cure for being a murderer.'

Investigative journalist Sadie Harrison, however, has suggested that Lauren Jones was a victim of a serial murderer who preys on young girls. In 2007, she wrote: 'Three girls were killed in eerily similar circumstances. Katie Masters, Lila Foster, and Lauren Jones were all murdered on the thirteenth of March – with years between them. Their bodies were decorated and posed in the same position. Police must explore a connection between them.'

The search for Mia Donovan continues. If you, or anyone you know, sees Mia, police ask that you call 999 immediately.

CHAPTER 8

JESSIE

Monday, 10th March

It's four a.m. and I've woken for the fifth time. Mark and I didn't watch a film last night. When he came in from the garden, he was in a terrible mood.

'Have you been smoking?' I asked him, hating myself for the accusatory tone.

He can do what he wants, really. It's just that it took him so many months to finally quit after fifteen years.

'No,' he said and, admittedly, he smelt of fresh air.

I smoked as a teen and I know how hard it is to get rid of the stench. He'd only been in the garden for a short while. Liza must've got it wrong.

He busied himself, rinsing out glasses and putting the plate from Mia's supper into the dishwasher.

'Are you OK?' I said. 'Did you find out who's been calling you all day?'

'Just some accident compensation company. Someone must've given them my details as a prank.'

'Who'd have done that?'

'I don't know, do I, Jessie?' he said. 'If I did, I'd have told you.'

He pulled out a chair and sat at the table, head in his hands.

'What's wrong?' I sat opposite. 'Is it because Liza's here? She'll be fast asleep by now. We can watch a film, like you wanted to.'

'I wish I hadn't answered the bloody phone,' he said quietly. 'I hate cold callers. And on a Sunday, too.' He stood, pushing the chair back loudly. 'Have we got any paracetamol? My head's killing me.'

'In the medicine box,' I said, not adding, *where it usually is.*

He shook two from the container and took them with a glass of water.

'I'm going to bed,' he said, kissing the top of my head. 'Why don't you put your feet up in the living room – watch something *you* want. Have a glass of wine.'

'OK,' I said as he walked out the kitchen.

It was half past eight in the evening and I was alone for the first time, but it didn't feel self-indulgent. I felt isolated. What was meant to be a nice day was spent with Mark's parents and my crying friend. The cherry on top was my annoyed, headachy husband. Drinking wine on my own was the last thing I wanted to do.

Now, with the sun close to rising, the lilac in the sky is visible through the curtains. I grab the sketch pad I brought to bed with me last night. I'd drawn idly with only the bedside lamp for light. Burning flames, sparks, fireworks, faceless eyes, shadow people in the distance. I haven't used it as a diary for a long time. Most of my recent commissions have been of children or animals. Light, happy.

Mark turns around in bed again. He's been constantly shifting round all night, and I'm exhausted. I seriously doubt the call he took last night was an accident compensation sales team – people get them all the time – but he was in such a foul mood I didn't want to press it.

It's rare that he lets someone or something else dictate his moods. I've known him for most of my life. He asked me for a date almost every day after my twentieth birthday. He waited for me when I was late coming out of art school, not wanting me to walk home alone in the dark. When I told him I wasn't ready for a relationship, he agreed to friendship. I don't know what gradually changed in me that I began feeling something more, but I remember him being away for a month with work and missing him terribly. He's always been my rock and I want to be here for him, too.

I'll wait to see if he wants to talk about what's bothering him. If he doesn't bring it up by the time he gets home after work later, I'll try to broach it. I hate confrontation, though. I physically shake at the thought of it. Too sensitive, my mum says.

Mark turns around again and I regret getting this new soft mattress. Every time he moves, I'm shaken. He wouldn't be enamoured at the thought of separate beds, even though I'd jump at the chance of my own *room*.

I've had six hours' sleep, which isn't too bad for me. Often, I like to paint in the quiet hours of the night when there's complete silence. I have a small room downstairs that looks out onto the garden. My studio in town is a wonderful space, but there's constant noise from people outside and the occupants of the flat upstairs.

My mind's racing too much. I open my side of the duvet and slide out of bed. I'll have a nice camomile tea; it might soothe the constant monologue in my mind.

Mark sits up as I reach the door, but his are eyes closed.

'It's not morning yet,' I say. 'You have a few hours until the alarm.'

The most delicious words to hear when half asleep, no doubt.

'You have it,' he says, eyes still closed. 'You can give it to me. I need it.'

He flops back down, and I open the door to the hallway. After briefly checking Mia's OK – she's sleeping soundly with her arms open wide – I head downstairs.

I push open the living-room door; I must've left the lamp on.

Liza's sitting in the chair by the window. She has one of our photo albums open on her lap.

'Liza?' I say. 'What are you doing?'

Though it's obvious what she's doing. I'd never dream of going walkabout in someone else's house in the early hours of the morning, let alone rifle through their stuff.

She turns a page.

'It's lovely that you have all of these,' she says. 'I don't have many pictures of me as a child. Mum said there was a fire and she lost most of them.'

'Aren't you tired?' I whisper in the hope she follows suit.

'I went to sleep so early,' she says. 'I've been awake since three. I'm sorry about coming downstairs. My phone ran out of battery and I didn't think to bring a charger, and I didn't want to put the telly on in case I woke you all.' She closes the album and gets up to put it back on the bookshelf. 'I'm sorry about being so drunk yesterday. I woke up feeling terrible about the things I said.' She walks towards me, her shoulders sagging. 'You will forgive me, won't you? I won't do it again. I'm not like that. It's just that I had a bad day, what with the falling out with Mum. It's always a bad time for her.'

I give her a light hug.

'Don't give it another thought. Do you want a cup of tea? I'm going to make one for myself.'

'No, I'm OK thank you. I've just ordered an Uber.' She

removes Mark's charger cable from her phone and heads to the hall. She sits on the bottom step of the stairs to put on her shoes. 'It should be here any moment,' she whispers. 'I'll head out now to wait for it. Thanks so much for having me. You'll have to come round to mine so I can return the favour.'

She gives a small wave before quietly opening the front door. She steps out and closes it carefully behind her.

What a very strange twelve hours these have been.

I'll never get back to sleep now.

I walk through the kitchen, open the door to my room and sit on the stool in front of my easel. I get my phone from the pocket of my dressing gown and tap out a short text to Liza, wishing her good luck for the interview, adding that she shouldn't give last night any head space; she's my friend no matter what. I used to drink too much alcohol in my twenties, and I'd have loved someone to do the same after me talking nonsense the night before. A decade of embarrassing weekends, but I can't undo them because I am who I am because of what came before now. Mark and I were just friends back in the 2000s, but he had his own problems. He didn't notice mine, however self-inflicted. He always says he was there for me, but he was too busy fighting off a woman who was *obsessed* with him. I still don't know her name.

I slip the phone back into my pocket and close my eyes as I listen to the sweet sound of birdsong outside. My early morning companions.

I remove the cotton sheet from the painting I've been working on for weeks. A picture of the girl whose face is embedded in my memory. Hair that's been lightened by the sun; freckles dotted across her nose. Headphones connected to a Walkman with an almost worn-out cassette of Take That.

Lauren Jones.

One day, she will get true justice.

* * *

I've lost track of time when I hear Mark in the kitchen. He's not trying to be quiet so his awful mood must've followed him into this morning.

He's flicking on the kettle as I walk in. It's only five thirty.

'Why are you up so early?' I ask him.

'I heard your friend leave,' he replies, reaching into the cupboard for two mugs. 'Did you check on Mia?'

'Yes.' I pull out a chair. 'She was sleeping; her arms were open wide like she was waiting for a hug.'

We both freeze.

Mark spins around.

I follow him up the stairs until we're standing over Mia's bed.

I release my breath.

She's lying on her side, breathing noisily.

I'm in awe, and grateful, that Mia can sleep through anything. I resolve never to allow someone I'm not a hundred per cent sure about to sleep under the same roof as my precious little girl. I don't know what I'd do if anything happened to her.

I take hold of Mark's hand and he gently pulls me out the door, closing it softly.

'Let her sleep another few hours,' he says. 'She gets grumpy if she has less than nine.'

'I know how she feels.'

We head back downstairs.

He finishes making tea and places one of the mugs in front of me on the table.

'Why can't you sleep?' he asks.

'I don't know.' I can't tell him it's because of his constant movement in bed and his godawful mood last night. 'Just thinking about last night. Are you feeling better?'

'It wasn't a cold caller.' He sits opposite. 'It was a debt

recovery company.'

'On a Sunday?'

'Those piranhas don't care what day or hour they call. They want to get you at your most vulnerable.'

He runs a hand through his hair, making him look even more dishevelled along with the shadows under his eyes and the stubble on his face.

'But you told them they had the wrong person, right?' I say. 'You haven't any debts.'

He stands and faces the kitchen window.

'It's my company,' he says quietly. 'I made a bad investment... borrowed funds from another business to complete the purchase.'

'What? You didn't mention any new investments.'

He might think I don't listen when he talks about work, but I take *some* of it in.

'I don't tell you about every single deal,' he says. 'You don't want to hear about boring contracts.'

'What did they say last night? How much do you owe? Your business is a limited company – surely you're not personally liable?'

He turns round, his eyes wide – a confused expression.

'I have a company of my own,' I say. 'I do most of my own book keeping.'

'You make it sound simple.' He paces the width of the kitchen. 'I need ten thousand pounds by the end of the day, or I don't know what they'll do.' He sits on the chair next to me, takes hold of my hands. 'They're not very nice people, Jessie.'

'Ten thousand pounds?' I want to swipe my hands away from under his. 'Where are you going to get that kind of money in such a short time?'

'We're married, Jessie,' he says. 'We need to work together on this. We need to keep us safe.'

'I haven't got that kind of money spare.'

'But your business has,' he says, standing again. 'You sold six paintings last month – one of them sold for five thousand pounds – the one that was featured in that magazine.'

'But I can't just give you all the money from my business account. I need it to pay the rent, more materials, lights, electricity, advertising. I need to take a wage. Wouldn't it be illegal to just hand it over to you?'

'We can draw something up – say your business is investing in mine. Yes. That would work. I can give you shares. It'd save you a fortune in Corporation Tax, too.'

'I can't,' I say. 'I'll need to talk to my accountant.'

'What?' He strides towards me. 'Can't you see how worried I am about all of this? For months I've tried to protect you from knowing about it – tried to deal with it on my own.'

'Can't you sell your car?' I ask. 'You're always talking about getting one of those electric bikes.'

He pounds the table with his fist.

'Jessie! Listen to yourself. This isn't some joke – it's totally serious.'

'I was being serious,' I say, leaning back, my heart thumping. I've never been intimidated by my husband before. 'Your car's worth treble that.'

'OK,' he says, calming slightly. 'I can sell my car, get something cheaper as a replacement. But that could take days. I need the money by the end of today. I could pay you back as soon as the car's sold. I promise. You'll barely notice it gone. I'll pay interest on top.'

'If they're threatening you,' I say, 'you should call the police. It's not right.'

'I've never asked you for anything, Jessie.' His arms circle, gesturing to the room. 'I've given you *everything*. You've never had a worry while you've been with me. Haven't I protected you for all of these years?'

'I know you have,' I say. 'You've always been there for me.'

'Remember what your life was like before we got together?'

'Yes, I remember.' I'm staring straight ahead. 'But I've done my best to forget. It's taken me years.'

'People used to post shit through your letterbox,' he says, walking towards me, standing over me. 'They used to shove you in the street.'

Adrenaline is making my hands shake, but at the same time I suddenly feel so exhausted I want to rest my head on the table and close my eyes.

I put my hands over my ears.

'Please don't talk about it,' I say, tears gathering in my eyes. 'What if Mia hears you? I *do* appreciate everything you've done for me. I love our life now. I don't want anything to spoil it.'

'Of course you don't. I'm always here to stop things upsetting you... turned over the television when there's something on the news... changed the subject when it's been brought up in conversation. Made up complete lies about where you were as a teenager.'

'Why are you bringing this up now? I *know* what happened to me – I lived it.'

'I'm sorry,' he says. 'You were just a kid. A different person.'

'What?'

'I'm emphasising – badly – that this is the time I need *your* help,' he says. 'And it's not as though it's something big. It's not as though I'm suggesting selling the house and moving away.'

'No,' I say. 'I meant why did you say I was *just a kid. A different person?*'

He rubs his forehead – the vein in his temple looks like it might explode.

'I'm not thinking straight, Jess,' he says. 'Let's talk about it later.'

'No,' I say, standing up. 'You think I did it, don't you?' I take a step back, away from him.

'No... I didn't mean it like that. I meant that everyone else thought you did.'

He reaches for my hand, but I keep it by my side, balling it into a fist.

'Come on, Jess,' he says. 'I didn't want to get into all of this. I know you didn't do it – you're not capable of doing something like that.'

'I told you I just found her like that.'

'I know,' he says. 'I totally believe you...'

'I can see by your face that you don't.'

His eyes are blank; it's a barrier he puts up so I can't read what he's thinking. He's used it so many times when he's told me little white lies.

But this isn't something small. This is huge. The foundation that my marriage is based on. He wouldn't have married me if he thought I was capable of doing such a thing.

'You think I blanked it out,' I say. 'Don't you? You think I did it – that I can't remember doing it.'

'No...' He rests his hand on my shoulder. I let it linger. 'I was just reminding you what I'd do for you. I was just hoping you'd help me get out of this. I'm really sorry, Jessie.'

I stand, still in a daze. I don't want to cry, but the tears spill out.

'If you think I killed her,' I say, looking into his eyes, 'then why did you marry me?'

I search his face for an answer, but I can't read what he's thinking. His eyes are bloodshot; beads of sweat are dotted on his forehead.

'I think I have my answer,' I say, walking shakily towards the door.

'Jessie, wait...'

He thinks I killed my best friend.

But I could never have hurt Lauren. Never.

I don't hear the rest of what he has to say; I slam the door shut and collapse into a heap on the hallway floor.

CHAPTER 9

SADIE

27 April 1996

Sadie Harrison – Freelance Reporter

Case: Rosie McShane (DoB: 29/01/1982)

Castleton Secure Unit, Merseyside

Length of time imprisoned to date: Seventeen months.

Notes:

Elaine Bushell is no longer the manager of Castleton Secure Unit. Her replacement, Geoff Rampling, reluctantly (*I don't understand the interest in her, personally.*) showed me to a kitchenette where Rosie was sitting. Her previously dark brown hair was dyed white-blonde and looked unwashed. There were dark circles under her eyes, and her dress had what appeared to be food stains down the front.

She stood when I entered. 'Would you like a tea or coffee?' she said. 'Geoff said I could make you a brew. We've got biscuits, as well.' As she started making the tea, Geoff wished me luck before leaving and closing the door.

'Why did he wish me luck?' I asked Rosie.

'Oh,' she said. 'He says that all the time. I don't think he likes working here.'

Time: 10.30

Sadie Harrison (SH): How have you been, Rosie?

Rosie McShane (RM): OK. I've had three blue in a row so I'm allowed to make you tea.

SH: Is that a rare thing – getting three blue cards?

RM: A bit. They're strict in here. You're not allowed to sleep in. And when I shove someone back, it's always me who's caught. I guess it's better than being a pushover. You can't stand out in here for being well behaved. It's not a good look.

SH: I suppose it's not.

RM: Thanks for your letter. I was trying to write everything down in reply, but I was afraid they'd read it before they posted it for me. I think they read every letter that goes out. Some of the other kids ask their friends and parents for all sorts – cigarettes, vodka hidden in squash bottles. As if they're not gonna get caught. (…) I thought you'd come back and see me sooner.

SH: I'm here now. You have other visitors, though?

RM: Yeah. (…) But you're the only one who doesn't talk like there's something wrong with me. Everyone stares at me like I've got two heads or something. Like I'm a monster. A few weeks ago, this woman visited – said she was an author. She wants to write a book about me. Do you think that'd be allowed?

SH: Who's writing a book about you?

RM: Her name's Felicity Fitzpatrick and she's quite posh. She doesn't sound as northern as you and me. She's probably from London.

*(**Note:** While typing this transcript, I discovered that Felicity Fitzpatrick's most recent articles have appeared in* The Sun *and the* Daily Mail*. In 1992, she published a book on Jack the Ripper, and in 1995, her book* Children Who Kill *reached number seven in the Sunday Times bestseller list. Rosie receives letters on a weekly basis from her, and has been told she will not profit from any percentage of royalties during her time here but is free to on her release.)*

SH: I don't know if that's such a good idea. She might write anything about you, Rosie.

RM: I don't like the name Rosie any more. I've been trying to get people to call me Angela, but no one's taking any notice. My new keyworker said I'll have a new name when I get out of here so I've been trying a few out.

SH: What do you like about the name Angela?

RM: It's from *My So-Called Life*.

SH: What's that about?

RM: Teenagers in America being moody and wanting boyfriends and girlfriends, mostly. It has Jared Leto in it. He's really fit.

SH: Is it suitable for a fourteen-year-old?

RM: I don't think anything in this place is right for a fourteen-year-old. You know the boys in here are terrible. They don't care.

SH: In what way?

RM: Taking the mick all the time, walking around naked. Setting fire to things.

SH: Have you mentioned it to your keyworker?

RM: As if that's gonna make a difference. It's the same everywhere. Greta Farley said the boys should be castrated.

SH: Do you know what that means?

RM: Yeah. Greta told me. She's been away for three years, but she's only been in this place a couple of months. She killed her dad, you know. The lads don't like knowing what she did. It scares them. They're extra cruel to her. Boys don't like girls who frighten them. Probably think she's gonna sneak in their room at night and murder them.

SH: Right. What do you mean when you say 'away'?

RM: Away from home.

SH: Does Greta ever think about what she did to her dad?

RM: I don't know. She never talks about it. We don't talk about things like that in here.

SH: What do you talk about?

RM: Music. *Hollyoaks,* things like that. Greta likes *Baywatch* because she likes Pamela Anderson. Have you seen it? It's pretty old now.

SH: Not a whole episode.

RM: We've watched *Grease* about a hundred times even though it's from the 70s. We do the songs outside as the lads take the mick when we do it in here.

SH: How is your education going?

RM: Why've you gone all serious? I was talking about dancing.

SH: Just wanted to make sure you were taking your subjects seriously.

RM: I don't get most of it. I can't concentrate. They get annoyed when I can't spell properly.

(...)

SH: Do you ever think about—?

RM: No. I told you last time, I don't want to talk about her. It makes me sad when I think about her. I was a different person back then. I would've stuck up for myself more if it happened now. No one took me seriously.

SH: How did you know what I was going to say?

RM: Because you left a long gap after I told you about the reading and writing. And because you did the same thing last time. If you ask me again, I'm gonna stop talking to you, and then we'll just be sitting here like a pair of idiots. Why are you trying to upset me? It's bad enough in here without you adding to it.

SH: Sorry, Rosie.

RM: Angela.

SH: Sorry, Angela.

RM: Your tea will be getting cold; you'd better drink up. I've not poisoned it or anything.

SH: OK.

RM: You looked well scared sipping that. I promise it's fine.

SH: It's lovely, thank you. Has your mum visited recently?

RM: Yeah, at Easter. She bought me this dress. Do you like it? I wear it most of the time.

SH: It's very nice.

RM: Do you think if this book – the one that Felicity Fitzpatrick is writing – comes out, I'll be able to afford more dresses?

SH: I hope so. When you get out, that is. Unless your mum gets them for you.

RM: God, I wouldn't let her have any of my money. She'd spend it all on herself. But if I save it up for when I leave this place I could train to become an actress. Or maybe a famous artist. Art's the only subject I'm good at and they make me draw all the time as *therapy*. Do you think they'll let me do that when I get out?

SH: (...) I...

RM: It's OK. You don't have to lie. I know they won't. No one would want to see me in a film or buy my paintings. The last man [name redacted] said I was a monster. No one would pay to see a monster unless it was crying or being stoned or shot with machine guns or sinking into quick sand.

SH: You're not a monster.

RM: Do you promise?

SH: I... Yes... I promise. I know you're not.

RM: Thanks, Sadie. You really are my favourite visitor.

SH: Just a quick question before I go.

RM: OK.

SH: Do you know someone called Lila Foster?

RM: I used to know a Lila but I don't know her surname. Why?

SH: Lila Foster was found dead a year before—

RM: No. She can't be dead. There was that time when she ran away from home, but I heard nothing about it after a few weeks.

SH: Did you have a falling out with Lila?

RM: Not a big one. She wasn't my friend anyway, not really. I only knew her for a couple of days.

SH: But you did know her?

RM: What are you trying to say? That I had something to do with it?

SH: I didn't mean to upset you.

RM: I didn't hurt her.

SH: I know you didn't.

RM: You believe me, don't you?

SH: I do.

RM: You're not kidding me, are you?

SH: I'm not.

RM: Thanks, Sadie. (...) Drink your tea up and I'll make us another. We still have ten minutes. I can eat at least twelve biscuits in ten minutes – I've timed it.

CHAPTER 10

HEATHER

I'm up before Eddie for a change, and I'm dressed and ready, sitting by the window waiting for my sister's car to pull up. I feel like I'm doing *her* a favour instead of her doing something nice for me. These bereavement groups are awfully depressing. I know that's a terrible thing to say, but my grief is always with me, constantly bubbling beneath the surface. Knowing others have been through similar experiences gives me no comfort at all. I don't need reminding that this world is a harsh and cruel place.

She pulls up on the road outside, gets out and opens the boot. Oh, God. She's dyed her hair a bright cherry red, and she's wearing an acid yellow jacket. We're not going to be invisible when we make our entrance into a room full of strangers, are we?

I open the door as she raises her hand to knock.

'Your hair!'

'Oh, don't,' she says. 'I left the dye on too long. You should see my bath. It looks like I've murdered someone. Didn't have time to clean it properly, so if something happens to me, and I don't make it home, tell them it's hair dye.'

She's always coming out with things like this. I try not to take offence.

'Tell who?' I say. 'And what's with the wheelie case?'

It's one of those plastic ones with a flashy neon pattern. She lifts it and puts it in the hall.

'I thought I might stay for a few days.'

'Oh, did you now?'

'You don't mind, do you?' She's giving me that twinkly smile, almost pleading with her hands. 'You said last week that I was welcome to come and stay any time.'

'People who say that don't actually mean it,' I say, half-joking. 'Not without at least six months' notice.'

'I'll take you and Eddie to The Silk Route to say thank you.'

'You've sold it to me,' says Eddie, appearing from nowhere, still in his dressing gown. 'Look after Heather, won't you? You know she doesn't like these things. She thinks they're depressing.'

'And *she* is right here, you know,' I say, stepping outside. 'I'll see you later, love.'

'I'll not eat lunch,' he shouts, 'so I can make the most of the meal out tonight.'

'He can't be bothered heating a tin of soup, more like,' I say after he's closed the door. 'It'll be more expensive for you staying at our house than being in your own home, what with that breakfast you promised me, too.'

'It's worth it,' she says, pressing her key fob, 'to spend time with my wonderful sister.'

'You're definitely after something.' I open the door to a pile of papers on the passenger seat. 'I suppose time will tell what that is.'

She reaches over to gather them, but not before I see a name on one of the files.

'Sorry, sorry,' she says, placing them on the back seat.

'Why have you brought those folders with you?' I get in. 'I hope it has nothing to do with where we're going today.'

'No, no,' she says, breezily, starting the car. 'Well, maybe...'

'You've been chasing down rabbit holes for years,' I say, sinking into the seat. 'You might just have to face the fact that—'

'She's innocent. I know she is.'

I look out the window as she pulls away from the kerb.

My sister is convinced that Rosie McShane is innocent. Over the years, she's tried to convince me of the same, but it's a hard pill to swallow. What if she's right and Lauren's killer is still out there walking free?

'We're not going to talk to her today, are we?' I ask, my heart racing at the thought. 'I don't think I'm ready for that.'

If I'm wrong, I'd feel an awful burden of guilt that I had a hand in her conviction. I've not seen Rosie since that day in court when she was sentenced. She looked so little, standing there, tears streaming down her face while she kept saying she didn't do it. Calling for her mummy, for her brother Billy.

A wave of something washes over me: panic? Doom? I don't know.

But my sister will find out the truth.

She's good at that. The famous Sadie Harrison, investigative journalist extraordinaire.

* * *

The breakfast was amazing: a non-greasy plate of sausage, bacon, two eggs, and a hash brown, but I wish we'd saved it for later so I'd have something to look forward to after this 'meeting'. And, delicious as it was, I can feel it churning in my stomach. We're standing at the bottom of the steps. The building looks like it was a church in the past, but now there's a poster on the noticeboard for an *Aladdin* pantomime that ended three months ago, and another advertising a production of *An Inspector Calls* by the Pimbo Players.

'Hello?' Sadie says to me.

'Sorry. I was miles away. What were you saying?'

I hate walking into these things for the first time. Everyone turns and looks, and I feel enormous pressure to tell my story to justify why I'm there. But I find it so difficult to share something so personal to people I don't know.

'There's no need to be nervous,' she says, taking the first step. 'They'll all be nice.'

'I don't think I can speak about Lauren today.' I follow her up the steps. 'And just because they're grieving, doesn't mean they'll be nice. One man once got so angry at the co-ordinator – who was, apparently, too condescending – that he flipped over a plate of biscuits.' I pull open the heavy door. 'They were those nice jam ones as well.'

'Anarchy.'

'It was, actually.'

Inside looks like any other public building. The walls are painted in thick yellowing white paint, the floor is grey linoleum. The large cork notice board near the entrance has too many flyers on it. The place smells of bleach and paper towels.

'Room three,' says Sadie, striding towards the door. 'We don't want to be the last ones in. I know how you hate everyone looking at you.'

'Then why did you bring me here in the first place?'

'For goodness' sake, Heather' – she shoves me in – 'will you stop complaining.'

It appears that everyone else was early. I check my watch: 10:01. The talking stops and every one of the ten people sitting in a circle turns to look at us.

My cheeks are on fire. I want to run back out, but it's too late. Sadie leaves me standing alone while she grabs two plastic chairs from the stack against the wall.

'Sorry we're late,' she says, her voice reaching the high ceiling. 'I thought it started at ten.'

'Not to worry,' says a man sitting with his back to the large windows. He's wearing jeans and a yellow T-shirt with a rainbow and the words *Rainy Days and Mondays Never Get Me Down* on it. 'I'm Clive. Help yourself to a tea or coffee.'

'We're OK for now, thanks,' I say, in case Sadie has other ideas.

The last thing we need to be doing is clanging about with cups and spoons with such a captive audience.

Chairs scrape as the circle widens for us.

I sit next to a young man who's wearing an anorak over a two-piece suit.

'Hello,' I say.

He presses his lips together in what I think is a smile and nods. He might be new, too. He looks as nervous as I feel.

'It's lovely to see we have three new people joining us today.' Clive smiles, his eyes crinkling at the sides. I think he's trying to convey warmth – a look I bet he's practised in the mirror. He opens his arms wide. 'Welcome.'

He gestures a hand to me, and I assume he's requesting my name.

'Hello, everyone,' I say, trying to sound as confident as I can. 'I'm Heather, and this is my sister, Sadie.'

'Hello, Heather,' says *everyone*. 'Hello, Sadie.'

This is all new to me. Usually there's no pressure or requirement to speak at the first session. Are we in the right meeting?

The man next to me shuffles about in his chair.

'I didn't think we'd actually have to talk straight away,' he says.

'You don't,' Clive answers. 'But if you feel comfortable enough to give your name, that would be lovely.'

'Uh,' he says. 'It's John.'

He says it so hesitantly; did he just give a false name?

'Welcome, everyone,' says Clive. He tilts his head to a woman on his right. 'Anita indicated to me earlier that she would like the chance to speak.'

The circle breaks into quiet applause.

Anita stands, takes a little bow, and sits back down. She's a small woman – looks like she's in her late forties. She must be a regular; she's wearing two scarves and fingerless gloves to shield her from this freezing cold room.

'Thank you,' she says. 'It's taken me four weeks of coming here, but I finally feel comfortable enough to share.'

We listen as Anita tells her story. She and her husband were driving home from a holiday in Cornwall. It was three in the morning – she'd already been driving for six hours – and she was tired. Her husband Alan was asleep. She kept meaning to pull off at the next service station to get a coffee and have a quick nap, but before she got there, she opened her eyes to find they were veering towards the hard shoulder. They hit a parked van at sixty miles an hour.

Everyone – including me – is shedding tears by the end.

'It's the guilt as well as the grief,' she says. 'I killed my own husband. The one thing that gives me comfort is that he was fast asleep and he didn't know about it. They said he would've been killed instantly – didn't feel a thing. But it doesn't help. It happened fifteen years ago and I still can't forgive myself.'

My heart skips a beat.

If I'd kept a better eye on Lauren; if I'd paid more attention when she came in to see me with the bunch of daffodils she left in a pint glass of water on the kitchen table. If we hadn't moved to that street. If I had told her that I loved her that day instead of shoving her back outside to play. If I had done just one of those things, my darling daughter might still be alive. She might have had a family; she might have been a successful businesswoman; she might've been a famous movie star. All those *might've-beens* turned into *never-would-bes*.

'Thank you so much for sharing that with us, Anita,' says Clive, after a respectful moment of silence. 'I think it's time for a pause. A comfort break and a coffee. We'll resume in ten.'

Sadie's first to the refreshments table. She pours us each a coffee, and I grab two biscuits to be polite. I follow her to the window and she places our drinks on the sill.

'See that woman over there?' She points with her eyes. 'The one in the black trousers and burgundy jumper?'

'Yes.'

'That's Kathleen Lewis. I've been trying to find her for months.'

'What? Why?'

'Now don't get cross with me, Heather,' she says, looking into my eyes. 'But you know I've been looking into other cases similar to Lauren's...'

'How you think there's some kind of serial killer on the loose, you mean? I told you. I just can't believe that. What happened between them was an isolated incident. They were best friends. Rosie was jealous. I don't even think she meant...'

Sadie narrows her eyes.

'You've forgiven Rosie?'

'I didn't say that.' I place the biscuits next to the coffee on the windowsill. My stomach is tight; I can't eat anything else in case it comes back up. 'She was twelve years old. A child. She's been punished for what she did. But what you're suggesting is so outlandish. That Lauren was in the same place as a serial killer who happened to be passing by at the very moment she was alone in that field. I really can't see it.'

'Everything about serial killers is outlandish,' she says. 'There's nothing normal about them. Two other girls – three if what that woman over there can confirm—'

'Sadie, please. I know you've tried countless times to convince me, but after the last time, you said you'd stop. Take your findings to the police. If they think there's a case, then I can begin to deal with it. Do you even have a suspect?'

'It has to be someone who knows Rosie. There are too many coincidences. First there was Lila...' She notices the tears welling in my eyes. 'I'm sorry, Heather. Sorry. I just want to get to the truth. For Lauren.'

'I saw her, Heather,' I say quietly. 'I saw Rosie kneeling next to her. There was no one else around.'

Sadie takes in a long breath. As she exhales, I realise she's trembling.

'That woman over there. Her daughter was twelve years old when she was murdered on the same day – the thirteenth of March. But this was in 2001.'

'God, that's awful. That poor woman.'

I briefly close my eyes and try to imagine how this woman heard the news. Or did she find her child herself, like I did? I grip hold of the cold radiator.

'This was when Rosie was in the secure unit. This girl lived only a few minutes away from where Rosie was locked up.'

'I know this sounds terrible, Sadie,' I whisper. 'But children are murdered more frequently than you think – well, than *I* think. It's more likely that this little girl was killed by someone she knew. It's tragic. It really is.'

'But Heather.' Sadie rests her hand on my arm. 'This little girl's hair was decorated with daisies and buttercups. Remember you went to find the flowers Lauren had in her hair, hours later in the dark with a torch and they were gone?'

'I don't want to think about it.'

'But this is why we're here. This woman – Kathleen – posted on a forum I've been following.'

I should be used to Sadie by now. Dragging me into her dramas for the sake of a story – when the truth is that Rosie was found guilty. I saw her with my own eyes. It's what I keep repeating to myself because the alternative is too upsetting. That two girls lost their childhoods on that awful day.

But there's a niggling doubt. The seed that Sadie planted so many years ago when she first started talking to Rosie. At first, Sadie said it was because she wanted to get to the truth of why Rosie had done it. Then, after the first visit, Sadie began to doubt the conviction. I've tried to block it out, but some of it has seeped in.

Oh, God. What if she's right? I'd never be able to forgive myself.

'I need to leave.'

I stride towards the coffee table, Sadie close behind.

'But we need to know. If Rosie didn't do it... There's been a serial killer for all of these years, targeting young girls on the same day. How many more are there that we don't know about?'

I place my still-full cup on the table.

'On the same day?'

She nods slowly. 'Four girls. All killed on the thirteenth of March.' She places her cup down, too. 'Heather, that's just two days away.'

CHAPTER 11

SADIE

29th January 2002

Sadie Harrison – Visitor

Rosie McShane (DoB: 29/01/1982)

Castleton Secure Unit, Merseyside

Length of time until release: 10 days

SH: Happy Birthday, Rosie! I can't believe you're twenty – it's making me feel old.

RM: Thanks, Sadie. You haven't recorded me in ages.

SH: I hope it's OK.

RM: I suppose. Do you think you'll still write that book?

SH: I'm working on something else at the moment, but if all that works out…

RM: Well the last one didn't work out, did it? With that Felicity woman. She said her publishers didn't like where she went with it.

SH: I think it was too soon.

RM: It was seven years ago. I can't believe how long I've been in here.

SH: Not long to go now, Rosie. Until you're free. Are you still going with the name Jessie?

RM: I think so. It sounds a little bit like Rosie. But even if I change my name, you can still call me Rosie. Or Jessie. Whichever one you want.

SH: OK. I like the name Jessie. It suits you.

RM: Thanks. I hope I get used to it. I've only been using it for a month. I worry that I'll turn around if someone calls out my real name.

SH: Maybe wear headphones.

RM: All the time?

SH: I was just kidding. Sorry. I hear they're going to organise a party for you.

RM: Yeah.

SH: You don't sound so excited about it.

RM: I like parties, but I'm a little scared.

SH: About being on the outside?

RM: Yes. I'm looking forward to the freedom. They've organised a flat for me. I haven't been alone for years. It'll take a bit of getting used to, not being watched all the time. It's like *Big Brother* in here. Have you seen that show?

SH: Bits of it.

RM: You don't watch telly much, do you? (...) Why do you look all nervous?

SH: I didn't want to bring all of this up on what should be a positive time for you, but...

RM: Go on.

SH: The police still haven't found who murdered Lila Foster.

RM: Oh. Do you still believe the person responsible for Lila's death is the same person who killed Lauren?

SH: I'm trying to piece things together. It's hard when there are no suspects on the police's radar, and Lila's parents won't speak to me.

RM: Perhaps you could talk to my mum. She might know more about it than I do.

SH: Your mum? Why?

RM: Because we were on holiday in Scarborough when we met Lila – not long before she went missing. I thought I'd already told you that when you mentioned her the first time. Mum's memory might be better than mine... Though, saying that...

SH: What?

RM: My mum's recollections aren't the best. She likes a drink. It wouldn't surprise me if that whole year was a blur to her.

SH: She's not returned any of my phone calls. Would you be able to put a word in for me? Tell her what I'm trying to do?

RM: If you pay her, she might talk to you. I'm not even joking, which is sad, but true. She'll speak about me to anyone if the price is right. I remember that interview she did for the *News of the World*. Proper sad face she had on her. I bet she got a few hundred quid for that piece.

SH: I'm sorry, Jessie.

RM: It is what it is.

CHAPTER 12

JESSIE

Monday, 11th March

I'm in my studio, sitting on a stool in front of a half-completed portrait of Stanley, a spritely Jack Russell with a mischievous twinkle in his eye. I've barely made any progress, but that's not surprising considering I've been replaying the conversation Mark and I had this morning.

Usually I can switch off when I paint, but it's not working this afternoon. I managed to put on a good show for Mia before school: putting on the radio to overcome my quietness as I made her breakfast; listening to her talk about her new best friend as she ate; driving to school instead of walking because I had to get to work.

It was made easier by the fact that Mark left earlier than usual. I didn't have to pretend that I'd forgiven him.

I'm exhausted. I couldn't manage even ten minutes' sleep after the row with him. I'm still in shock that he said those things to me. He's been in my life for over twenty years yet deep down he believes I'm some kind of monster who could kill her best friend. Why were people so quick to believe it was me? I still don't understand it. I've tried to bury the hurt, the frustration. The loss of all those years stolen from me. I thought I'd done a good enough job until Mark brought it up again. The one person I trusted in the world. My protector, my partner. Who actually believes I'm guilty of killing another human being. Though, not just any human being. Lauren Jones. We were best friends from the age of four, after she moved in next door. The sister I never had. We did everything together. She was so pretty – she didn't realise how lovely she was. We were boy crazy and music mad. Almost every Sunday teatime we would sit in her bedroom with her cassette player to record the charts, trying to cut out the DJ talking with varying degrees of success. I don't think we ever listened back to those tapes, now I think about it.

I wipe the tears that always come when I think too much about her. I feel terrible for mourning the loss of my childhood years when Lauren had hers stolen from her. She didn't get the chance to leave school, to meet someone and fall in love. To perhaps have a family of her own. Like I did with Mark.

I hadn't seen Mark since *before*. After I was released, I saw him loitering outside the first flat I was placed in, which was over fifty miles away from where I grew up. He was sitting on a bench near the row of steel-shuttered shops where teenagers used to hang around, smoking cigarettes.

I was heading out to meet my first probation officer and was wearing a hat and sunglasses. I was petrified that someone would recognise me – that they'd follow me, shout abuse or push me in front of a moving car. My imagination was far worse than my reality.

My pathetic disguise was obviously not good enough because Mark recognised me straight away.

'Rosie,' he said, standing up. He grabbed a bunch of flowers off the bench. 'I've been waiting for you. I wasn't sure if I'd got the right address. I didn't write it down.'

'Do I know you?' I asked, staying twenty feet away, not recognising him.

My heart was pounding. What if there was a knife hidden in those flowers – or maybe poison that you breathe in? I stepped backwards, looking round. I noted two women sitting at the bus stop, and a police car in the distance. But I knew as much as anyone that bad things can happen in daylight if someone was fast enough.

'My name's Mark,' he said. 'I'm good friends with your brother, Billy. We went to the same school.' He stuck a hand in his pocket, shifting his weight between his feet. 'I was a few years above, though. Do you remember that time I came to Scarborough with your family? In your stepdad's static caravan by the sea.'

'Mark...' I said, trying to get a good look at him but it was hard to see through sunglasses on such a cloudy day. I took them off. It had been almost eight years since I last saw him and he looked so different. He was only fifteen, then, and now he was twenty-four – four years older than me. 'Yes. I remember that holiday. He wasn't my stepdad, though.' I hadn't thought about *Uncle* Davy in a long time. 'Billy hasn't mentioned you for years; I didn't think you two were that close any more.'

'We are.' He took a step forward. I took another step back. 'I got your address from your mum. She wouldn't have given it to me if I were a stranger, would she?'

'She gave you my address?' I felt tears springing to my eyes, though I shouldn't have been surprised. 'Just like that? She knows it's meant to be a secret.'

'She said you could do with a friend. She said you were really lonely around here, not knowing anyone. Especially after being in prison so long.'

'It was a secure unit.'

'Sorry,' he said, suddenly looking nervous. 'That's what I meant. Sorry.'

'It's OK. It's the same thing, probably.'

He looked at the road ahead, then at the woman walking on the other side of the road. Everywhere else but me. Was he scared? Did he think I'd kill him? We'd not spent much time together as kids. I was the little sister: ever-present but easy to ignore.

'Was it awful in there?' he said eventually.

'Of course it was awful,' I replied. 'It wasn't a holiday. I was in there for seven years.'

'Right. Yes. I'm sorry. Again.'

He placed the flowers back on the bench.

'I'll just leave these here. I've put my address and phone number on the card in case you feel like talking to someone. We could chat about anything you want. Your mum said you liked art and drawing and stuff. My grandma gave me a watercolour set once.'

'Really?'

'Yeah. When I was about ten, but...'

I pressed my lips together to stop them from smiling.

'Right. OK.' He started to walk backwards. 'Bye, then. It's nice to see you, Rosie.'

'I'm not Rosie any more,' I said quietly. 'I'm Jessie.'

He bowed his head slightly.

'Nice to meet you, Jessie. I hope I see you again soon.'

Once he was out of sight, I approached the flowers, tentatively searching for something that shouldn't be there. I checked my hands for signs of a reaction in case he'd laced them with some sort of poison that seeped through skin. Yes, I was being overcautious, but they warned me at Castleton to be careful. I needed to protect my new identity as much as possible. It costs a fortune, apparently, to set people up with somewhere to live, and to issue them new official documents. They didn't want to have to keep doing it. *For your sake as well as ours.*

I took the card attached to the flowers. *Mark Donovan.* He

didn't live in Clayton any more, which was a relief. Now he was in the next town – such a coincidence. I thought it was fate. I didn't know where I was going to live until the week before I left the secure unit.

When I got home, I telephoned my mother and indeed she had given him my address. She said that Mark was still in contact with Billy. Either it was an elaborate scheme that fooled my mum, or he was actually who he said he was. After my mum gave me a detailed description – including the quiet tone of his voice, and the way he brushed his long fringe from his eyes, I finally believed it was the latter. We've been in each other's lives ever since.

Fast forward to now and neither of us have seen my brother Billy for years. I don't think he approved of me and Mark getting together. He vaguely tried to advise against me marrying him the day before the wedding, but I thought he was supposed to do that in the absence of any father figure.

Billy lives in Scotland now, but it may as well be the other side of the world, the amount of times we've seen each other. He's only met Mia on a handful of occasions; each time bringing her a soft toy. She has a little row of them along the side of the bed, lined up in a specific order that has to be right before she goes to sleep.

My precious Mia. I would hate it if she found out what happened to me, to Lauren. She's too young to understand any of it. Too young to understand that people would be horrible to me – and to her – if they found out that I was found guilty of murder. I have to protect her for as long as I can. Thinking about Mark letting it slip like he did this morning – when Mia could have heard – makes the ball of fury turn in my stomach. How dare he? Is it too much to ask that we try to give Mia the best childhood we can?

A door slamming in the flat upstairs shakes me back into the present.

Now – my mind in the studio where it's supposed to be – the paint's almost dry when I go to dip my brush in it. This is the problem with acrylics. For the quick turnaround needed for this piece, I can't use oils – sometimes they take weeks to dry.

I glance at my phone. No missed calls from Mark, and it's two thirty. He usually phones me at lunchtime. I had hoped he'd call to say he was sorry, that he didn't mean any of those things. That it was the stress of the loan company that's getting to him.

The loan company. We hadn't really discussed details of that, had we?

Was he using my past as a distraction?

Mark uses distraction all the time, but it's usually over trivial things. When I asked him last week why he'd left his dirty trainers in the kitchen, he replied that he was just about to get us a nice takeaway. Ignoring my question with a reply that cancelled it out.

My phone rings.

'Mum,' I say, putting on a jolly voice. 'At last! I thought you'd gone into hibernation! Did you get the flowers I sent you?'

'Yes, yes,' she says quickly. 'They were lovely. Enough about me. God, I can't imagine what you're going through, Jess. Have the police been keeping you updated with their search? You have to keep on at them. I hope the community are rallying around you. There's a train that'll get me into Cheltenham at about six p.m.'

'What?' I look at my phone to double check I'm talking to the right person. 'Mum, what the hell are you talking about? Why would you come down here? You said you hate trains.'

'Mia, of course. It's all over Facebook that she's been kidnapped. Oh, God, Jessie, I can't believe this is happening. My one and only grandchild. I need to be there for you.'

She sniffs and lets out a small cough, trying to hold back the tears.

'What?' I slide off my stool, walk into my small gallery. 'I'm not on Facebook or any of the others. Mia's at school. I dropped her off as usual this morning.'

'But it's been shared about a hundred times,' she says. 'All around the country.'

'That can't be right.' I put on my jacket and grab my keys. 'But I'm heading to the school.' I step out, close, and lock the door. 'I'll ring you as soon as I know more.'

'OK, Jessie. Breathe, breathe.'

'I am, Mum. I'm running.' Where the hell did I park my car? 'I'll call you when I find out more.'

There it is.

My hands are shaking as I press my key fob.

I pull out as fast as I can without knocking someone over.

This has to be a joke. Some sick joke.

Everything will be fine.

I hope to God Mia is OK.

CHAPTER 13
SADIE

5th June 2003

Sadie Harrison – Freelance Journalist

Jessie S. (Formerly Rosie McShane), age: 21

Location: [redacted], JS's new residence.

Notes:

Jessie's flat is extremely neat and tidy. It's sparsely furnished with one settee, a dining chair and table, a small bookcase, and a large television in the corner. There are two framed photographs in the bookcase – one of her mother, another of her brother Billy. Her hair is dark brown and long. She's wearing glasses – the first time I've seen her with them.

Time: 17:45

Sadie Harrison (SH): Recording started.

Jessie S. (JS): I can't believe it. And so close to me, too.

SH: It's an awful situation. I feel terrible for Katie's parents and her little sister.

JS: I can't stop thinking about it. Especially because it happened on Lauren's anniversary.

SH: Have the police talked to you about it?

JS: You mean have they searched my house because they think I killed someone else?

SH: Don't be like that, Jessie. You know I didn't mean it that way.

JS: It's what I felt when my probation officer came round. I could tell they thought it was suspicious that she – Katie Masters – went missing soon after I was released, even though I wasn't even in the county. People will never forget, will they? Even though I have a new name, a new life – I can't escape what happened.

SH: They'll catch the person responsible, Jessie. They'll have evidence, maybe DNA these days. People around here don't know who you used to be.

JS: What if he comes after me – sets me up again?

SH: But you weren't in the area when it happened. And I'm not one hundred per cent sure it's a male.

JS: Really?

SH: I can't rule out the possibility it's a woman, but you'll be safe. Your identity is protected. No one I know – other journalists, I mean – has any idea where or who you are now. I've tried to throw them off a bit, given them false snippets.

JS: Thanks, Sadie.

(…)

SH: I like what you've done with the place. It's very tidy.

JS: Well, I haven't much stuff, so…

SH: Does it feel good to be out?

JS: For sure.

SH: Isn't it how you expected it to be?

JS: It's hard being away from home, my brother, and my mum. But everyone around there knows who they are. I can never go back there.

SH: Are you upset your mum didn't move down here to be close to you?

JS: I don't know. I've learned not to expect too much from her. I'm twenty-one now. (…) There's one person from Clayton who's been good to me, though.

SH: Who's that?

JS: Mark Donovan. He was good friends with my brother when we were growing up. Don't think he sees Billy much. Though *I* don't see

Billy that much, either. My brother's always travelling. I think he's in Birmingham at the moment.

SH: When did he come back into your life? Mark, I mean.

JS: About a week or so after I got out.

SH: Ah, OK.

JS: You sound apprehensive.

SH: I don't know him.

JS: I didn't believe he was who he said he was when I saw him again – he looked so much different. I thought he might've been a reporter trying to get a story. But I asked my mum and she backed him up. She said he was all right, but not to let him bother me if he becomes too much.

SH: Why would she think Mark would bother you?

JS: I didn't want to ask. Sometimes what people say about other people isn't always true.

SH: Don't you trust the opinion of your own family?

JS: I do. But they don't come to see me often. They've been here five times. I mean, I know my mum doesn't have much money to travel and all that, but I've been here for a year.

SH: Do you wish you could see her more?

JS: I know I was just complaining, but I think it's OK the way it is. She likes to be on her own. When we were kids, Billy and I used to have to get our own food, our own shopping. Billy used to find money that Davy lost down the gaps in the sofa. When Billy got older, he managed to find odd jobs, cleaning cars and stuff, and he'd buy us a loaf of bread, some butter, and baked beans. He didn't have to share it with me, but he did. I think he spent most of his cash on fags and lager, though.

SH: That sounds awful.

JS: I thought you knew about all of this. Didn't I talk about it before? When I was a kid?

SH: Not in so much detail.

JS: You shouldn't feel sorry for me.

SH: I can't help it. You could've had such a different life. (...) Why are you crying, Jessie?

JS: The way you just said that. I wish my mother was more like you. More compassionate. Sometimes I think she believes that I did it – even though she said she was convinced I was innocent. I think she was lying to me. I hate it when people lie to me.

SH: Oh. (...) I need to tell you something.

JS: What?

SH: I didn't tell you when we first met in case you wouldn't speak to me.

JS: What is it? You're scaring me.

SH: It's nothing to be scared of. It's just that...

JS: Go on.

SH: It's not the reason why I've been coming to see you over the years, but… God, this is harder than I thought it would be.

JS: Just say it, Sadie.

SH: I'm Lauren's aunt.

JS: What? Laurie… Lauren Jones's aunt?

SH: I'm so sorry. I should have told you years ago. Lauren's mum was so desperate to know why you did it – she said that if she knew why Lauren was killed, then she'd get some peace. But before I even came to see you, I doubted your guilt.

JS: Why hadn't I met you before? I mean before everything happened.

SH: Did Lauren introduce you to any of her other relatives?

JS: I don't think so. I can't remember if I did. How is Lauren's mum?

SH: We don't see each other on a daily basis. She doesn't agree with what I'm doing… Well, actually she doesn't know. She still thinks that you…

JS: Oh. Right. I don't blame her.

SH: Are you OK? You don't look OK.

JS: I had no idea. I feel terrible. I hope I didn't say anything bad against Lauren when I was younger. I didn't know what was happening, not really.

SH: Do you understand why I didn't tell you who I was? That you were too young to understand when I first came to talk to you. I don't want you to think there was some conspiracy against you.

JS: I can't believe you don't hate me. Did you hate me when you first met me?

SH: No, Jessie. Not at all.

JS: And you really believe I'm innocent? You're not lining me up for some big revenge plot?

SH: No, of course not. Do you believe *me*?

JS: I think so. Do you think Lauren's mum will ever believe I didn't do it?

SH: I can't lie to you, Jessie. I don't think she will. I'm sorry.

JS: It's not your fault.

SH: No. It's the fault of whoever is doing this to little girls. And I'm determined to find him.

JS: So you *do* think it's a he?

SH: I do. And I'm going to try my very hardest to hunt the bastard down.

CHAPTER 14

HEATHER

I wish Eddie were here because sometimes I feel a bit awkward talking to strangers. He's great at filling conversation gaps with small talk. Thankfully, the busyness of this café is a distraction from the silence between Kathleen and me as we wait for Sadie to order the coffees. Luckily we're next to the window; Kathleen's obviously not one for chit chat either.

'Sorry about the wait.' Sadie places the tray onto the table. Today's proving quite expensive for her. 'There's only one person serving, and it's lunchtime for goodness' sake.'

She pulls out a chair, sits next to me, and hands out the coffees.

'I need to be leaving in ten minutes,' says Kathleen. 'I'm looking after my grandson.'

'That's nice,' I reply, feeling a familiar pang of envy. 'How many grandchildren do you have?'

'Three. All boys. All completely different.' She smiles as she pours a little milk into her drink. 'Thank God I have those kids, you know. I thought it would get easier losing Paige, but it gets harder when I see my other kids reaching milestones she never had the chance to.'

'Lauren was Heather's only child,' says Sadie, and my face flushes.

'It's not a competition,' I say, quietly.

'I'm sorry to hear that, Heather.' Kathleen looks right into my eyes and like a shot I feel the connection between us. Of grief, pain, guilt. 'Sadie told me what happened to Lauren.'

I take a side glance at Sadie.

'You were in the ladies',' she says quickly.

'It's some consolation for you,' says Kathleen, 'that they caught who was responsible. A shock, though? That it was her friend.'

'A terrible shock,' I say. 'It was like I saw my daughter's last breath, but in reality I knew she was already gone when I got there. And Rosie McShane was just sitting there. No remorse, no sadness. She was just staring at Lauren, curiously. It was so strange. Like she'd been taken over – like she wasn't really there.'

'Where is she now?' Kathleen asks. 'The girl – Rosie, I mean. Is she still in prison?'

'Lord, no.' My eyes flick to the sky like they always do when I talk about her. It's a habit. I hate saying her name, though I can feel Sadie's gaze. I know what she's thinking. 'She was released over twenty years ago. Got given a new identity – a new life.'

'Have you seen her since?'

'No, but her mother still lives in the same area. She has the sense to keep out of my way. Hardly leaves the house, so I've heard.'

Sadie taps on her mobile phone – she's itching to press record, I know it.

'Sadie thinks Rosie McShane didn't do it,' I say. 'She thinks there's a serial killer out there who's targeting young girls.'

'Heather!' says Sadie. 'You can't just blurt it out like that!'

'But Kathleen only has ten minutes – even less, now. We can't sit here skirting around the subject.' I look at Kathleen –

she's frowning, confused. 'Did they catch the person who killed your daughter? Sorry, what was her name again?'

'Her name's Paige, and no they didn't. A man confessed to it, but they realised that he was lying.'

'Why would someone lie about that?' I ask.

'He was already in prison – thought he'd get special treatment or something. I've no idea.'

'Your daughter went missing in March 2001,' says Sadie. 'Is that right?'

'Yes, but she wasn't found until three weeks later.'

Kathleen's eyes fill with tears.

'We don't have to talk about this, do we, Sadie?' I am almost pleading. 'We're upsetting her.'

'This was when Rosie was in the secure unit. You and Paige lived only minutes away.'

'I don't get where you're going with this—' I start.

'I think it was someone who has a connection to Rosie,' Sadie interrupts, looking intently at Kathleen. 'Was there something about Paige's murder that newspapers didn't write about? Something unusual, but they didn't want it leaked because only the murderer knows about it?'

Kathleen looks at me, at Sadie.

'Why would you ask that?'

'It wasn't mentioned in court,' Sadie explains, 'but when Heather found Lauren, she had flowers in her hair. Like a decoration of sorts.'

Kathleen pushes her cup away.

I half-expect her to get up and leave.

She turns to face me.

'Dried buttercups and daisies.' Kathleen takes out a notebook, scribbles her number and rips out the page. 'I'm sorry, I really do have to go. Call me when you get a chance and we can talk more.'

'OK,' says Sadie.

Kathleen stands.

'It was good to meet you both. I'd do anything for Paige to get justice.'

I wait until Kathleen has left before I say, 'Why didn't you prepare me for all of that? Why didn't you tell me about the flowers in that poor girl's hair?' I look out the window. Kathleen's standing as though paused, staring at the clouds. 'I don't understand how someone else could've done it, Sadie. I was right there – I saw Rosie kneeling over her. There was no one else in sight. I heard Lauren scream.'

'But what if it wasn't Lauren's scream – what if it was Rosie's, and she'd just found her best friend lying there? If you hadn't seen her, no one would've believed that Rosie had killed Lauren.'

'You're saying that it's my fault?'

'No, of course not.'

'Certainly sounds like it.'

Sadie takes hold of my hand.

'What are the chances of an unconnected case where a twelve-year-old girl is also found dead with flowers in her hair? Three of the girls had connections to Rosie. We need to find out if she knew Paige, too.'

'And how are we going to find that out?'

'I'm going to ask her.'

CHAPTER 15

JESSIE

By the time I get to school, several parents are already standing at the gates. It's almost half past three; Mark's mum is meant to collect her today, but she's nowhere to be seen and I can't see her car on the street.

I race to the office and am breathless when I knock on the window.

'Is Mia still here?' I ask. 'Mia Donovan in Reception.'

The woman – I think her name's Jackie – stares at me quizzically.

'Did she have a medical appointment?' She picks up the clipboard and runs a finger down the list of names of children who arrived late or left early. 'Her name's not here. Is everything all right?'

'My mum said she's been taken,' I hear my voice trembling; my whole body is trembling. 'Please, can you tell me if you saw her leave?'

'No, I didn't,' says Jackie. 'But I don't watch the gate. It would've been noted on the CCTV if a child left – we have to buzz them out with a parent or guardian. And there's nothing here. Who told you she was missing from school?'

'My mum. She said she saw it on Facebook. I know it sounds strange.'

'I'll phone the class. See if she's still there.'

She turns her wheelchair to the side and picks up the telephone. It takes what feels like forever for her to place the handset back down.

She's smiling. A good sign.

'She's fine, Mrs Donovan,' says Jackie. 'She's just putting on her coat along with the rest of the class.'

My knees feel weak with relief.

'Thank you so much, Jackie.' I want to hug her. 'Thank you, thank you.'

She moves closer to the window.

'Some people use social media to find their estranged families by putting missing posts on there,' she says gravely. 'Report it to the police if there is someone trying to find you... You know... if there's an estranged biological father no longer on the scene. It's happened where there's been instances of domestic violence.'

'I...' The Reception door flings open on the other side of the playground and Mia is one of the first to come out. 'Thanks so much, Jackie.'

Mia's eyes rest on me, then they focus on a figure to her right.

Oh great, it's Judith. Never one to miss a commitment, but then why should she – she didn't know I'd be here.

She's striding over to me, holding Mia by the hand.

'Well, this is a lovely surprise,' says Judith. 'Did you manage to get off work early? How lovely. I know *I* wouldn't be able to concentrate if I had to work through school run time.' She visibly shudders. 'I couldn't bear it.'

'What?' I say, holding my hand out to Mia and she takes it far too quickly. 'No, I didn't just pop out for the school run, Judith. I ...'

It's not worth going into detail. The drama of it all would send her into a panic and she's not my mother's greatest fan as it is.

When Mark and I first got together, she wasn't *my* biggest fan, either. Mark always said she was fine with what happened to me, but it was only after Sadie Harrison – the journalist I used to talk to – spoke to her that she began to realise I was innocent.

I often wonder what Sadie's doing now. The last time I spoke to her was just over four years ago when I called to tell her about Mia being born. I didn't think to ask her to update me on her investigation. If she had important news, she would've told me.

'You look miles away,' says Judith. 'Are you poorly?' She moves her face closer to mine. 'You do look a bit peaky. Do you want me to look after Mia at yours? You could have a lie down. I could make you some of my bone broth.'

I visibly shudder.

'Thank you so much for the offer, Judith, but I think I'll be OK. I'm sorry that you've had a drive out.'

'That's all right,' she says. 'Now that I'm close to town I could do with a trip to the garden centre. My lavender needs repotting. It's surprising how quickly it grows, you know. But it's so worth it for the smell, don't you think?'

'Yes.'

I keep getting jostled by kids eager to get home, but Judith doesn't seem to notice.

'Thanks again, Judith.' I start edging away. 'See you soon.'

We rush to the car; I'm scanning the streets for someone who doesn't belong in this setting – someone who wants to take my child.

But I have no idea who I'm looking for.

* * *

We've only been home ten minutes when Mark's car screeches onto the drive. He flies through the door, down the hall and into the kitchen. He runs straight to Mia and grabs her in a hug that covers most of her face.

'Daddy,' she says into his jacket. 'You're too early. It's normally teatime when you're back.'

'I thought I'd surprise you,' he says, releasing her. 'But while I get changed, could you watch a bit of telly and have a snack?'

'OK, Daddy,' she says, pulling out her chair and sitting at her little table. Mark gets her a packet of crisps and a juice. 'Thank you. Mummy doesn't let me have crisps after school.'

'Just this once, then,' Mark says, grabbing her iPad and placing it down as a makeshift babysitter.

Mark pulls the kitchen door ajar and we go into the living room, standing at the furthest point near the window.

'Has she been OK?' he asks. 'Did she pick up that there's something wrong?'

'No, but it's been hard to pretend things are normal.'

Mark takes off his jacket and drapes it along the back of the sofa.

'I'll go and get my laptop from the car,' he says. 'See what else we can find.'

I look out the window. There are no unfamiliar cars lurking outside and the street is empty of people – they're all at work except for Mr and Mrs Grantham who live opposite. They've been retired for years and if anything suspicious were to happen, Mr Grantham would be the first to spot it.

Mark comes back in carrying his laptop case. He places it on the coffee table, and we sit side by side on the carpet.

'I haven't logged onto Facebook for months,' he says, navigating to the site. 'Glad it's remembered my password.'

There are loads of red notifications on the top right of the screen.

'Over two hundred, Mark,' I say. 'I didn't know you were that popular.'

'I'm not,' he says wryly. 'Most of them are about nothing. Here we go.'

He clicks one of the notifications. It opens with a picture of Mia in school uniform, and the post:

Mia Donovan age 4. Missing from home. Please share so we can find her.

'What the hell?' he says. 'Someone has tagged me in this. It's been shared all over the country.'

'Who wrote it? They haven't said much.'

I move closer to the screen to look at our daughter's smiling face. It's the same photograph we have on the bookcase, but we never share her pictures online. Not even as a baby.

'I have no idea.'

He clicks onto a Facebook page entitled:

Help Find Mia Donovan

'The admin is listed as a John Smith, but that won't be their real name, will it?' he asks.

'I doubt it. Who do you think's behind it? Is it those people who are after you for money?'

'I can't think of anyone else who would do this.'

Mark slumps back against the bottom of the sofa. He rubs his forehead.

'Shall I contact Sadie?' Her name pops into my head for the second time today.

'Who?'

'Sadie Harrison,' I repeat. 'The reporter who believed me.' I sound like I've reverted back to childhood. 'I mean the investigative journalist. She'll be able to do some digging.'

Mark sits up straight.

'We're not contacting some nosy hack, Jess,' he snaps. 'She probably made up a story about there being a serial killer out there to get on your good side.'

'No, she didn't.'

'Well, where is she now, then?' he says, echoing my previous thought in the school playground. 'This "Sadie Harrison".' He makes quotes with his hands. 'If she was so convinced of a killer on the loose, she'd be still working on it, but she isn't. She probably wasn't even a real journalist.'

'What? Of course she was. Why are you questioning it now? They still haven't caught Lauren's killer, Mark.' I take several deep breaths. I need to be quiet, stay calm. 'Don't you ever wonder if he'll come back?'

Mark tilts his head to the side.

'The police think they've solved Lauren's case, Jessie,' he says, his tone gentle. He takes hold of my hand and squeezes it softly. 'I don't mean to sound crass and dismissive, but this has nothing to do with Lauren Jones. We need to pay them the money, Jess.'

His phone vibrates in his pocket. He takes it out and reads the message.

'Shit,' he says. 'Look.'

He hands me the phone. It's another message from an Unknown Number.

> Send the money or I will tell the world about your wife. Your perfect life isn't so perfect after all, is it?

'I knew it,' I say. 'I told you. It's all connected.'

Bile rises to the back of my throat.

I need to stand. I need air.

I rush into the hall to open the front door and step outside.

I swallow the nausea, but grip onto the wall to steady myself.

'Are you OK?' Mark steps out and puts an arm around my shoulders. 'I can't believe all of this is happening. I'm so sorry, Jess.'

'How would they know about me? On my studio website, I'm not recognisable. There are no photos of me online – I check every week without fail.'

'They might not know anything – they might be bluffing.'

'It doesn't sound like they're bluffing,' I say. 'Putting missing posts online, then hinting that they know what happened thirty years ago. Mark, if anyone finds out, people will never believe I was innocent. It was hard enough convincing your mother. We'd have to move. I can't have Mia growing up knowing her mother was in prison. She's too young to understand anything like that.'

'If we pay the money, Jess' – he glances at the living-room window to check Mia isn't watching – 'then they'll stop. The only reason they're doing this is for the money.'

'What if it's not them – what if it's someone connected to Lauren?'

'For the tenth time, it's nothing to do with Lauren,' he says almost through gritted teeth. He's losing his patience with me. 'Say there was some random killer on the loose, they wouldn't want to draw attention to themselves like this, would they? After getting away with it for thirty years.'

'Mia's only four years old.' I say, covering my face with my hands. 'If anything happens – if he comes for her – I don't know what I'd do. She's everything to me.'

Mark puts his other arm around me.

'I...' he starts.

But he doesn't finish.

He doesn't believe Mia's in danger from a random child killer. He thinks I'm making the whole thing up.

I stand straight, take in a lungful of cold air, my eyes watering.

'OK,' I say flatly. 'I'll transfer the money to your account so you can pay them. Maybe it's best if I go and stay with my mum for a few days until this has all calmed down.'

'I think that's a good idea.' He follows me back into the house. 'Is your brother there... to keep an eye on you all?'

'No, he's still in Scotland.'

'Then perhaps I should come too, to—'

'I'd rather it just be Mia and me. You need to sort out the mess you made. You can contact the school, the police, and explain everything to them. Straight after you've returned these people's money.'

'OK.'

'You can drop us at the station,' I say, looking at my phone. 'There's a train in an hour.'

I book the tickets, then ring the bank to transfer the funds from my business account into Mark's.

I take a look at our lovely living room, our lovely kitchen, before heading upstairs to pack. I'm not a hundred per cent sure I'll ever see it again.

CHAPTER 16

JESSIE

This is not the first time I have had to flee. A year before Mark and I became a couple, I was studying art at Lancaster University. I lived on a lovely little street with two other young women who were in some of my classes. One of their friends – I think her name was Hayley – was studying criminology and I knew as soon as I met her that I'd have to be vigilant when I was around her – never relax, never join in when they had a drink while watching *Blind Date* on a Saturday night.

Hayley got drunk one night two months later and told me she had been reading about children who murdered other children. She told me about Rosie McShane – told me things I didn't know because they weren't true at all. A few days later, and after a call to my contact at the police, I was transferred to Liverpool John Moores University and set up in a flat close by. I was alone, again.

And here I am once more.

Mia was wary when I told her we were going away for a few days – she doesn't like missing school. I convinced her that she'll have lots to talk about when she gets back, and now she's wearing her earphones, watching her iPad because she got bored of seeing all the green fields. I hope she'll be OK at Mum's. We've always stayed in hotels when we've visited before.

It's almost five thirty and we're pulling into Birmingham New Street. Mia pulls down her headphones so they're resting on her shoulders.

'Are we having tea on here?' she says. 'Can we go to the café?'

'When we get moving again,' I say. 'Lots of people will be trying to find their seats.'

'It's too busy on here, Mummy. Will Daddy be OK on his own? Can we ring him when we get to Manchester?'

'Course we can. And Daddy will be fine.'

She rests her head on my shoulder. She always gets sleepy when we're travelling, but this time I don't try to keep her awake. I put my arm around her as I look out the window at the people queueing to get on the train. We're all going in the same direction, but all with completely different lives. As usual, I scan for anyone looking straight at me. Nobody is.

My phone buzzes. It's a message from Nicola Parry, my liaison officer at the police. I haven't needed to speak to her since Mia was born. Even though Mark wouldn't want me telling her about our financial affairs, I had to. I open her text.

> Hi Jessie. The Facebook posts have been taken down. There's no evidence the person or persons have knowledge of where you live. We are trying to find out who created the page. Will keep you informed. Stay vigilant and contact me or dial 999 if you feel in immediate danger. Safe journey.

She's to the point as usual. No pleasantries. But I relax a little more knowing she's taking my worries seriously. At least someone is.

Now Mark's paid back the money, I'm praying nothing will

come of this horrible situation, and the Facebook posts will stay deleted. He managed to get the company's assurance that they'd take them down, but they're hardly the most honest of people. What was Mark thinking getting caught up in something like that? Why did he need money so badly that he'd go to a loan shark? He didn't actually tell me it was a dodgy loan, but it's pretty evident.

I need to stop thinking about it all. As the train sets off again, I look down at my daughter. Her eyelids are flickering as she's drifting off to sleep. She's in her own little world.

My world was so different when I was her age. If we'd had phones and iPads back then, would we have been less inclined to play outside all day? We seemed so much younger than kids do today. Some of my classmates still played with Barbie at the age of eleven, for goodness' sake.

It's hard to believe that I was once Rosie McShane. She feels so detached from me: the little girl who found her best friend lying dead in a field; who screamed for help, and when that help came, was accused of hurting Lauren. I wish I'd never found her. No one believed I didn't do it. Even some of my family members couldn't look me in the eye. Psychologists agreed I was a cold-hearted killer, jealous of her best friend, but I wasn't. I was in shock. Just a child. The trial was a blur to me. It was like they were talking about someone else.

Most of the other children in the secure unit weren't like me. They were proper hard, tough. They smoked cigarettes and didn't care if the adults caught them doing it. They answered back; they took no crap. They believed I did it, too. Said they locked their doors at night in case I suffocated them in their sleep. None of *them* had killed anyone – well, except for Greta. Their crimes were drug dealing, assault, armed robbery. A right merry bunch, as you can imagine. And all of them said they didn't do it, too. I wasn't anything special thinking I was innocent. Everyone did.

Sadie Harrison was the only one who talked to me like I was a normal person. She was curious. Asked curious questions about my childhood and the people around me. Mark never met her. I'm sure he thinks I made her up. Sadie had told me to be wary of him because he seemed to latch onto me. She said he might not have the best intentions. I'd hoped I had proven her wrong, but now I'm starting to doubt it.

For the first time in years, I google her name. There are several articles that link to her blog. The most recent is dated November last year. *Seven girls still missing nationwide: their families deserve answers.* I skim the post and scroll to the linked articles at the bottom. One of them seems to jolt my heart. Despite my weekly searches, I've never seen it before.

Rosie McShane: an innocent childhood lost.

Tears spring to my eyes.

I wasn't imagining it. She really does believe me.

* * *

I'm weary from the two-hour train journey, but after a nap, two hot chocolates and a KitKat, Mia is as bouncy as Tigger.

'Hold on to the handle of the suitcase, Mia,' I tell her. 'It's too busy for you to be wandering away from me.'

We stop near WH Smith, trying to keep out of the way of impatient travellers.

'I'll just get out Gran's address,' I say. 'There are usually taxis outside railway stations.'

'I like taxis,' says Mia. 'Are they those big black ones? I've never been in one of those before.'

I try to memorise Mum's address before slipping it back in my pocket: '...44 Glen Eldon Drive. 44 Glen Eldon Drive...'

'That sounds like a pretty road,' says Mia.

'Here's hoping.' I grab hold of the suitcase. 'Let's go.'

Outside, there's a long queue at the taxi rank. Thankfully there seems to be a quick turnaround, but I've a fizzing in my stomach; a slight dread of reaching our destination. Mum has lived in her latest house for just over a year, but I've yet to visit. Some of her dwellings in the past have not been the best, but she still lives in the same area as where we grew up. God knows why.

Lauren's parents probably moved away decades ago. Mum and I never talk about them. I can barely think of them without welling up – without picturing Heather and Eddie mourning their daughter, living with their sadness. It's almost thirty years ago to the day. The thirteenth of March is only days away.

I blink the tears away. This is why I try to block everything out because it simmers just beneath the surface. Mum doesn't like to talk about the past, either. It's like a line was drawn in the sand when I came out of Castleton, and I stepped over it into a new life. She's very good at compartmentalising things – living in the present.

God, I hope she doesn't get embarrassingly drunk in front of Mia. Last time, she tried to hide it by drinking in mugs, but she couldn't hide the slur in her voice when it came to night-time. But it was OK because it was Christmas and Mark was drinking, too. We stayed at the Premier Inn down the road. The place she lived in then was a lovely new build, but she shared it with that layabout lodger she called a boyfriend. There was no way I'd be taking my child there now if they were still together. But really, what choice do I have? It's not as though I have loads of friends to go to, and Liza has her own troubles she's dealing with.

We're at the front of the queue. I yank open the door to the empty black cab, throw the case in and place Mia's rucksack on the floor.

'In you go,' I say, lifting Mia inside.

She scrambles onto the seat, and I climb in next to her.

I give the driver the address, and we pull away from the kerb. We've travelled miles, but I don't want the journey to end. I wish we could just stay in limbo, my daughter and me.

'Don't forget the seatbelt, Mummy,' she says, looking worried.

'Thanks, love,' I say. 'I don't know what I'd do without you.'

* * *

We stop outside a small bungalow, which was not what I was expecting at all. The grass in the small front garden is overgrown; the only one on the street that isn't manicured to perfection. I feel a wave embarrassment and I'm not proud of it.

I hand the driver a twenty-pound note, inwardly cringing at having to wait for the change. I can't afford to throw money around after Mark borrowed most of my company's funds. I've only two weeks' wages left in there.

I step out the cab, and the driver doesn't help with my bags. I don't blame him.

'Come on, Mia,' I say as she slides off the seat. 'We're here.'

I help her out, and she stares at the house, squinting in the dimming daylight.

I slam the door. The bloke drives off without saying goodbye.

'Charming,' I mutter under my breath as I shove the rucksack onto my shoulder.

'I'm scared, Mummy,' says Mia. 'It looks spooky.'

I glance at the house – the curtains are closed, and the windows look as though they've not been cleaned in years.

'It'll be OK.' I take hold of her hand for my sake as well as hers. 'Come on.'

The wheelie case catches on the uneven weed-strewn path as we head to the door.

'Give it a knock, Mia,' I say. 'Make it as loud as you can in case Gran's asleep.'

'Does she go to bed early?' she asks. 'Is it because she's old? Raine at school said her great-grandma used to be tall and now she's half the size.'

'Raine?'

'Yeah. There's Raine and there's Summer, but they don't like each other.'

'Sounds about right.'

Mia forms a fist and punches the door three times.

'Your grandma's not *that* old that she's started shrinking,' I say. 'At least I don't think so. It's been a year.'

After a few seconds, there's still no answer.

I bend to peer through the letterbox.

'Hello? Mum?'

She'll tell me off for being impatient, but I can feel the panic in my chest. I hope she hasn't passed out.

I stand and dab my forehead. When did it get so hot up north?

There isn't a gap in the curtains to peer through so I try the handle on the door.

'Thank God for that,' I say, pushing it open.

'Don't swear, Mummy.'

'That's not swearing. I'm literally thanking God.'

Twenty per cent of what I say to Mia stretches the truth.

'Daddy says you don't believe in God,' she says, following me inside.

'Well, Daddy doesn't know everything.'

I feel a tinge of disloyalty. I shouldn't pass my anger at him onto our daughter.

I close the front door, with just the right amount of force to announce our entrance but not enough to scare Mum. The hallway carpet is worn to the underlay in places, but it's been hoovered. Shoes, folded towels, and a bottle of Flash are on the hall table. I hope we're in the right house.

'So you *do* think God is real?'

'Not now, Mia. Mum?' I shout. I don't want her to think she's being robbed. Three years ago, she said a bloke came through her back door and she almost swiped him with the kettle. 'Are you in, Mum?'

I have no idea if this is a shoes-on or shoes-off house. It changes with Mum's mood. I keep them on. A breeze runs into the hall: fresh air mixed with cigarette smoke. I follow the scent to the kitchen where the back door is open.

Outside, on the tiny patio area, Mum's sitting on a white plastic chair, puffing on a cigarette and flicking through a TV magazine. She looks up at me and her shoulders jolt back.

'For fuck's sake,' she says. 'You scared the shit out of me.' She bends to pound the cigarette on the ground, stands and flings the magazine onto the chair. 'Why didn't you use the doorbell?'

'I didn't see a doorbell.'

'So how did you get in?' She sways a little, but her focus is sharp.

'You left the front door open.'

'Mummy?' Mia appears at the back door.

'Who do we have here, then?' Mum says, stretching out her arms. 'Are you going to come to Grandma?'

Mia's bottom lip quivers and she looks up at me, concerned.

'Maybe just shake her hand for now, Mum,' I say.

'Shake her hand? The world's gone mad.'

Mia holds out her right hand and shakes Mum's.

'I suppose that'll do for now.' Mum squeezes past Mia to get inside. 'Would you like a cup of tea, young lady?'

'She doesn't drink tea or coffee.'

I guide Mia into the front room. It has a beige leather sofa and a brown chair with wooden arms and legs. There's a flatscreen telly in the corner on top of a small glass table. A couple of photos hang on the wall above the gas fire, framed in wood – the same IKEA-style frames I had next to my bed as a teenager at Castleton.

'Wait there a sec.' I hand Mia my phone. 'Play whatever game you want while I talk to Gran.'

Gran, Grandma, Granny. I have no idea what my mother wants to be called these days. The last birthday card she sent Mia was signed with her name.

In the kitchen, Mum's pouring boiling water into two cups.

'Do you still take three sugars?' she says.

'No.' I am trying to keep my voice steady. 'Not since I was a kid.'

'Ah. I see.'

'But I'll drink it,' I add,' I don't mind.'

'Dare say you need it,' she says, bashing the teabag on the side of the cup with a spoon. She lifts it out and dumps it in the sink. 'You've lost weight since I saw you last. When was that?'

I stand aside as she reaches into the fridge for the milk.

'Over a year ago, I think. The Christmas before last.'

'Not as long as I thought, then.'

I try to see inside the fridge for signs of booze, but she's too fast. She pours two dashes of milk and leaves the carton on the side.

'Did you find out who was behind those Facebook posts?' she asks.

'No, but I've let Nicola know.'

'Still Nicola, is it?' She takes a sip of hot tea. 'I'm surprised she still works there, the high turnaround they have these days. Not the easiest job, being a police officer. Not that I know any, of course.' She wrinkles her nose. 'Bit strange, the whole thing, isn't it? Did you think someone had found you?'

'Yes,' I say. 'I always think someone is going to find me.'

'You can't live your life like that, Jess – it's still so weird calling you Jessie. I don't think I'll ever get used to it.' She sighs. 'I've always wondered why you didn't move abroad. I'd have loved to visit you somewhere sunny. Cheltenham's a bit, you know...'

'What?'

'They're a bit well-to-do around there,' she says. 'I wouldn't fit in at all. Anyway...' She puts the milk back in the fridge. 'No one's found you in years. They take it a lot more seriously since Mia was born. It's not just you they need to protect.'

A postcard on the back of the fridge catches my eye. It's probably from my brother Billy. Even though he sees Mum even less than I do, he's still the favourite. I don't question it any more. The last time I saw him was when Mia was around two years old, when he'd just started a new contract on an oil rig off the coast of Scotland. He looked completely different: weather-beaten, a beard, long straggly hair.

'You know Billy's engaged now, don't you?' says Mum. 'To a woman called Saskia.'

'That's nice. I didn't even know he'd met someone else. The last time I spoke to him he was with a woman called Grace.'

'He met Saskia online, I think. She's from Sweden. They've got a child on the way.'

'What?'

'I think he wanted to tell you in person.'

'I hardly see him,' I say. 'At this rate it'll have been born next time he visits.' I sip the too-sweet tea. 'Anyway. How are you? You look good.'

Her hand runs through her hair.

'My roots are due a retouch, but I've started using a mois-turiser. Sandra next door recommended it to me. She used to be an Avon lady, rep or whatever they call it these days, and she has loads of samples. And I mean loads. They're probably decades old but they smell all right. She's given me all sorts. I think she feels sorry for me, being here all on my own.'

'That's nice of her.'

Mum leans against the kitchen counter.

'What's up with you?' she says. 'I've never heard you be so dull. Nice this, nice that. What is it?'

'I've had a terrible couple of days. Mark had some trouble with a business associate. And then you called to say my child had been snatched. It's all been a bit too much.'

'Hmm,' she says, narrowing her eyes. 'What kind of trouble? I've never figured out what Mark does for a living.' She grabs her packet of cigarettes and stands by the back door. 'But you don't need unnecessary hassle. You've dealt with too much in your life. If you get a divorce you'll get half of everything – and half the trouble. Because that's what men are. A whole lotta trouble.'

'That's a bit of a stretch, Mum.'

'Sandra next door has a son who works for this lawyer lady. Proper posh, she is. Saw her name in the paper when they were reporting that body in the suitcase trial. Did you follow it?'

'What?' I'm blinking, trying to take in the flood of information. 'No. I don't really follow the news about murders. I don't need to seek out awful things. They seem to find me often enough.'

She takes a long drag on her cigarette and shakes her head slightly as she blows it out.

'I haven't had a drink in six months,' she says. 'I know what you're thinking.'

'I wasn't thinking that at all.'

'I go to a meeting most days,' she says, gazing out at next door's back garden, which is bursting with colour. It's probably Sandra's, whoever she is. 'It's a bit religious, but I just go with it.' She glances at me. 'I'm sorry, you know. They tell us we should apologise for the way we've treated people in the past.'

'What are you sorry for?' I ask, but to be honest, it could be for a whole host of things.

'It's just that *my* mum...' She throws the half-smoked cigarette into a long-neglected bird bath. 'No. I shouldn't make excuses. I'm not a child any more. I have my own agency.'

'What?'

She shakes herself out of her daydream,

'I tell you, Jess,' she says, smiling, closing the door. 'They're rubbing off on me. I think it's actually a cult. No one talks about it outside those four walls. If you see someone you recognise you have to pretend you know them from somewhere else. Like prison, I suppose.'

She places her hands on my shoulders.

'You're so beautiful, Jessie.' She wipes a strand of hair from my face. 'And such a gentle soul.' Her eyes fill with tears. 'And I'm sorry for not being there when you needed me. I will do my best from this day forward.' She rolls her eyes. 'Oh my god, I'm doing it again.'

'Have you ever thought of amateur dramatics?' I say.

I hold my breath; the silence between us is like a ball of energy.

She presses her lips together before she bursts out laughing.

'You know what, Jess,' she says, 'I think you're onto something there.' She grabs a packet of party rings from the cupboard. 'We used to get these at Christmas. They used to be your favourites. Do you remember?'

'I do.'

'You used to lick and lick and lick the top till the icing came off.' She shakes them onto a plate and arranges them icing side up. 'You were a strange kid, Jess.'

I follow her into the living room.

'You're one to talk,' I say, and she laughs again. 'Can you show me the Facebook post you saw? Mark and I looked yesterday but when I checked on the way here, I couldn't find it. Nicola said they'd managed to take it down, but I want to be certain it's not still circulating.'

She sits in the armchair and crosses her legs.

'You're not one for small talk, are you, Jessie?' She swipes a biscuit from the plate and dunks it in her tea. 'Not in front of the little one, eh?' She shoves half the biscuit into her mouth. It's still crunchy and the sound of her chewing it goes right through me. Finally, she swallows. 'We'll talk about it when Mia's asleep. Don't want to scare the poor thing.'

Mia's eyes widen.

'Grandma's just joking,' I say. 'Here, have one of these. They're biscuits with icing on.'

She takes one from the plate and places it on her lap.

'Grandma makes me sound old,' says Mum. 'Call me Marie.' She slurps her tea and makes a sigh of satisfaction. 'Don't suppose you've got any cash on you, Jess? We could order a pizza. I'll pay you back so it's my treat.'

'I'll get it, Mum,' I say. 'As a thank you for letting us stay.'

'See' – she sinks back into the chair – 'I knew there was a reason I had kids.'

She winks at Mia, and Mia looks as though she's about to cry.

Which makes two of us.

CHAPTER 17

SADIE

8th August 2003

Sadie Harrison – (SH) Investigative Journalist

Interview with Marie McShane (MM) Rosie's mother

Location: 17 Bramwell Street, Clayton, Manchester.

Time: 15.30

SH: It's recording now. Thanks so much for talking to me, Marie. I've been trying to get hold of you for ages.

MM: I'm a hard person to track down (laughs). I move house a lot. I get itchy feet if I stay in one place too long. We agreed a hundred quid, yeah?

SH: That's right.

MM: I really appreciate that. And any follow-up interviews will be the same?

SH: Of course.

MM: I wish I'd known that earlier (laughs).

SH: If you're uncomfortable answering any of these questions, please don't feel obliged to answer.

MM: Don't worry – I don't do anything I don't want to (laughs).

SH: Can I ask why you chose to stay in this area? I know you've lived at several addresses, but they've only been a few miles away from each other.

MM: Why should I leave? I haven't done anything wrong. If I moved to another county then people would be suspicious, wouldn't they?

SH: Why would they be suspicious?

MM: I dunno. I think people blame me. They always blame the parents for what their kids do, don't they?

SH: What was Rosie's childhood like?

MM: I'm not the best person to ask, am I? It's hardly objective.

SH: I don't need objective – I want your opinion.

MM: I did the best I could. Ask anyone. I worked nights a lot of the time – first at the pub across the road, then at the old people's home, though I don't think you're supposed to call them that any more.

Back-breaking work it is – even at night. That's when most people die, you know. They told us to go for a ciggie break at 3 a.m. for that very reason.

SH: Who looked after Rosie and Billy?

MM: In the early days, sometimes next door would keep an ear out; sometimes Eva from the house opposite would sleep in the armchair. She didn't mind. It gave her something to do because her grandchildren were all grown up. It was a different time back then. People would do things for each other, you know? (...) Don't I know you? Your face looks familiar.

SH: I covered Rosie's trial in court.

MM: You sat next to Heather Jones, didn't you?

SH: And what about the later days? Who looked after your children, then?

MM: What do you mean?

SH: Never mind. How long were you sitting on your doorstep?

MM: Dunno. I liked to sit there on Sunday afternoon. Couple of lagers, a packet of fags. While away a few hours. It's nice being outside – you don't feel as alone.

SH: You could see the entrance to the field from your house, is that right?

MM: Yeah.

SH: Did you see the girls go in?

MM: Yeah. They were with that other girl. Rosie told the police about her at the time. Didn't know her that well, myself.

SH: Samantha?

MM: Yes, that's right.

SH: The police said they didn't speak to the girl – or if they did, they didn't make it public what she told them. Are you certain you saw her?

MM: As certain as I can be.

SH: Did you tell the police you'd seen her?

MM: I probably did. The whole ordeal was a blur.

SH: Did you see anyone else go into the field, or anyone else come out?

MM: I'm just going to top up my drink, hang on a sec.

SH: OK.

(...)

MM: Sorry about that.

SH: I asked you if you'd seen anyone else going in or out of the field.

MM: Oh, right, yes. No, I didn't. I would've said it at the time if I remembered that.

SH: Where was your son?

MM: Billy? He was in his room. He'd been to Blackpool with his friend. Went to the Pleasure Beach.

SH: What time did he get back?

MM: About midday. His friend Mark drove them. They stayed overnight, went on the Saturday.

SH: What's Billy doing now?

MM: He lives in Birmingham – got himself a job in engineering, which is amazing considering he left school without any O levels. He's thinking about moving to Australia once he's saved up enough cash.

SH: What was Rosie like as a child?

MM: You're all over the place with these questions.

SH: Sorry.

MM: Are you trying to confuse me on purpose?

SH: Not at all.

MM: Rosie was like any other twelve-year-old. Played out with her friends, watched *Grange Hill*. She used to love going to the library on a Saturday to borrow those *Sweet Valley High* books, but after she started high school herself, she wasn't interested in reading. Maybe if she had... I still have some of her old books, I think. Few photographs, too. She doesn't want them any more, but I kept them in case she changes her mind.

SH: Do you think I could take a look at them?

MM: Some musty old books? I put them in the loft. It'll be a right pain to go and get them. I tripped up outside the Co-op the other day. Right did my ankle in. I took pictures of the bruising – here, have a look. I've put a claim in with the council but Shay next door said it could take years to get my compo. If I get anything at all, the tight, thieving bastards.

SH: I could have a look for you. I can give you an extra twenty pounds for the trouble.

(…)

SH: The time is now 16:30. Thanks, Marie. I'll return them when I've had a read through. Are you sure she won't mind?

MM: Yeah. She's never asked for them back, so I doubt she'll notice. Not that she comes to visit. I have to traipse all the way over there if I want to see her.

SH: I just have a few other questions if you don't mind. Do you have any connections to Scarborough? Did you and Rosie visit there at all?

MM: We've been on holiday there a few times. My ex Davy Tetlow had a caravan over there. Proper nice, it was. He was a lovely man. Why?

SH: There was a girl who went missing in 1993. Lila Foster. Did Rosie know her?

MM: She might've played with her once or twice. I didn't pay much attention to be honest. The kids used to just go off all day.

SH: She was found dead several weeks later.

MM: Oh. God, that's terrible.

SH: So you were at the caravan park in Scarborough around the time Lila went missing?

MM: Where did you hear that?

SH: I just put two and two together. Did the police question you and the children after Lila went missing?

MM: They might've done. There was nothing to tell them. Davy was with the boys. Think he took them fishing while Rosie helped me pack.

SH: So you *do* remember that day?

MM: Bits of it. Just because I didn't hover over the kids like parents do these days, doesn't mean I didn't look out for them. I love my children. I might not have been the world's greatest mother, but I did the best with what I had.

SH: I didn't mean to upset you.

MM: I'm not upset.

SH: I'm just getting a few facts together. Coming back to Samantha. Can you remember what her surname was?

(...)

MM: I've no idea. Her grandmother Sylvia still lives round the corner. Samantha is Sylvia's daughter's kid so they won't have the same surname. Can't remember what number her house is, so you'll have to do some knocking on doors. Do you think Sam had a hand in what happened to Lauren? Rosie told the police all about her, but they pretty much ignored it. They thought she was deflecting – trying to pin the blame on someone else.

SH: I think it's something worth exploring.

MM: What's the point of all these questions now, though? Lauren's case is closed – Rosie's done her time. The police won't be interested in rehashing it.

SH: I just want to help the families find answers.

MM: But I don't know what all this has to do with Rosie.

SH: I think it was a coincidence that it was Mother's Day on the thirteenth of March in 1994 when Lauren was killed. As you know, Lila Foster disappeared on the thirteenth of March 1993, and then another girl called Katie Masters went missing on the same date in March this year, 2003. She lived on the same road as Rosie did when she first left Castleton Secure Unit.

MM: That's awful, Sadie. Their poor mothers. (…) I've not met many people called Sadie. Are you sure you're not connected to the Joneses? Why did you mention Mother's Day? Everyone knows the date changes every year.

SH: Who's that picture of… the one on top of the television?

MM: What? Oh, that. It was New Year's Eve the year before Rosie went away. That's me, Davy, Billy and his friend Mark. I remember they used to sneak some of the vodka when they thought we weren't looking. The pub was closed that year because Kenny the landlord and all of his staff were ill with food poisoning after Brenda didn't cook the turkey all the way through. It's one of the only photos that came out all right from that camera film. Can you see Rosie just behind the boys? The only kid who liked an ice cream cone in winter. It was just about to fall onto the carpet. Isn't it weird knowing that? Like being a time traveller. The dog licked it all up, and poor Rosie was distraught because it was the last one.

SH: That's Mark Donovan? The one Rosie's been seeing?

MM: I don't think she's seeing him. He popped round when Rosie first got out, but I don't think they've seen each other since.

SH: Ah, I see.

MM: Has she mentioned him to you? I don't want her hanging round with him. I thought it was weird him asking for her address to start with. What does he want with Rosie? I don't like that at all.

SH: I thought he was good friends with Billy – you took him with you on that holiday to Scarborough.

MM: That was a long, long time ago. A lot has happened between then and now. He's not the best person for Rosie. Billy fell out with him around five years ago.

SH: Do you know what they fell out about?

MM: Some girl, probably. Girls or money – that's how it usually is with lads, isn't it?

SH: I guess…

MM: Rossetti – that's her name!

SH: Whose name?

MM: Sylvia – Samantha's grandmother. Sylvia Rossetti. Must be in her nineties, by now. If you get along quick-smart, you might still catch her alive (laughs).

CHAPTER 18

HEATHER

We pull up to my house after travelling in silence for the last part of the journey. I admit to be quietly fuming that Sadie kept me in the dark about what she'd been working on. Especially because it was about Lauren.

'It wasn't that I hid it from you,' she said. 'I just wanted to be a hundred per cent certain before I shared my findings with you. It's taken me years to piece together a fuller picture. I've spoken to dozens of people over the years – people I don't think the police took the time to interview. And it's probably for the best that I tell you and Eddie at the same time.'

Now we're back at mine, I have a sick feeling in my stomach. I can't believe she's made me cast doubt on the original police investigation. Our Family Liaison Officer, Christina, who was here day and night supporting us through everything, was a godsend. I can't imagine them getting it so wrong. They were so sure of Rosie being guilty – there was no one else in the picture. I feel like half my life has been based on a lie. I could sleep at night knowing my daughter's killer had been punished for her crime.

Eddie opens the front door as we walk up the path. He's wearing his smart jeans and the red and black checked shirt he saves for special occasions.

'Sorry, Eddie,' I say. 'We're getting a takeaway instead. Sadie's got something important she wants to share with us.'

He stands aside to let us in.

'Eh?' he says. 'I had a bath and everything. I was really looking forward to it.'

'Sorry, Ed,' says Sadie, grabbing hold of her wheelie case's handle – it's still next to the front door. 'This is more important. You can order two starters as well as a main if you like. Will that make up for it?'

'And a couple of those nice bottled lagers they do?' he asks, following us into the kitchen-diner.

'Knock yourself out,' she says, reaching into her pocket for her phone. 'Use my Deliveroo account. Just make sure to change the address.'

Eddie takes the phone and almost jogs to the living room.

'I'll be back in a sec,' he says. 'I like to take my time with these things – make sure I weigh up all the options.'

'You don't have to pay for it,' I tell her. 'You bought breakfast, and you wouldn't take any money for petrol.'

'It's OK,' she says. 'I'll tell my accountant it's a travel expense.'

'Oh,' I say. 'Right.'

She heaves the case onto the table and unzips it.

'I thought you'd have more clothes than that if you're staying,' I say, seeing only one change of clothes, underwear and her PJs crammed into the mesh part of the case. In the main section are bundles of paper in buff folders, an A5 notebook in a polythene pocket, and an old tape recorder.

'What's that for?' I ask. 'Are you going to record us?'

'No,' she says, taking it out. 'I've got some old tapes of Rosie from when she was a child. I thought I could go over them – see if I missed anything. I've got headphones, so you don't have to hear her.'

'I might have a listen,' I say, sitting down. 'It'd be like hearing the past. I wish I'd taken more videos of Lauren. We only have that one from her tenth birthday party. And that's covered in snow we've played it so many times.'

'I can get it converted to digital for you,' she says. 'They're really good at correcting things like that these days.'

'That'd be lovely, Sadie.'

I glance across at the photo of Lauren on the back wall. She's smiling enigmatically – a Christmas fairy at her last nativity at primary school. She hated wearing that outfit, which was made from white netting and silver stars, complete with a lit-up sparkly tiara. She said she was far too old to be pretending to be something that wasn't real. She looked like an angel.

'Right,' says Eddie, returning with the phone. 'I've made my decisions. Thanks for this, Sadie, love. Do you want your usual chicken tikka, Heather? What will you be having, Sadie?'

'Sit down, will you, Eddie,' I say. 'Just put us down for a banquet for two.'

I feel a flash of guilt when I see his face almost crumple. It's not his fault my sister has been going behind our backs.

'Sorry, Eddie, love,' I say, reaching over to touch his hand. 'I didn't mean to snap.'

'What's wrong, Heather?' he says, pulling out a chair. 'Should I be worried?'

I don't know how he's going to take it. He's believed Lauren's death has been avenged, too. That he could grieve for her knowing that Rosie was never going to live a normal life again. But now we have to tell him that's not right at all – if what Sadie has discovered is true. The person responsible for taking our Lauren away has not only been living a life of freedom but has used that freedom to kill other innocent children. Destroying lives wherever they go.

My breathing is getting more laboured. The more I think about the implications of this, the harder it is to prepare myself for Eddie's reaction. I wish I didn't have a hint of what Sadie's about to say.

'Sadie,' I say. 'I know you've put a lot of work into all of this, but...'

Eddie takes hold of my hand and I squeeze it tight.

'You're scaring me, love,' he says. 'Are you all right? Has something happened? You've not sneaked off to the doctor's without telling me, have you? You've not had bad news?'

'It's nothing like that,' I say. 'You'd be the first to know if there was anything wrong with me.'

'Eddie,' says Sadie, still standing. 'You know I used to talk to Rosie when she was in the secure unit? You and Heather wanted to know why she did it, but she could never explain – in fact she kept denying ever harming Lauren. So I kept going to see her, see if I could find out anything else – to build up a picture of the people around her, of what actually happened that day.'

'Of course I remember,' he says quietly. 'It keeps me up at night thinking about it – why my daughter had to die like that.'

'And the flowers in Lauren's hair,' continues Sadie. 'We always wondered why that was hardly ever mentioned. Probably because by the time Lauren got to hospital, most – if not all – of them had fallen out.'

'But what's this got to do with now?' says Eddie, looking at me pensively. 'Is it because it's the thirtieth anniversary coming up?'

'I've been researching similar cases,' says Sadie solemnly. 'I found two other girls, both of whom went missing on the thirteenth of March. One was a girl called Lila Foster, who disappeared in 1993, another was Katie Masters who went missing in 2003. Both of them had connections to Rosie in some way.'

'But Rosie would've only been ten years old in 1993.'

'Yes, I know. I'm not saying she had anything to do with hurting Lila or Katie,' says Sadie, taking out the notebook. 'There are mentions of Lila Foster in Rosie's diary.'

'How on earth did you get hold of that girl's diary?' says Eddie.

'Marie let me borrow a box of books she was storing for Rosie,' she says. 'Years ago.'

'She just let you have them?' says Eddie, his eyes glimpsing at the ceiling in exasperation. 'God, that woman. There isn't a caring bone in her body, is there?'

'She's had a hard life,' says Sadie.

'And most of her troubles are caused by her own hand,' says Eddie. 'Don't tell me you feel sorry for her.'

'I don't know,' she says. 'I try to keep a balanced view.'

'Balanced?' he says. 'Her daughter killed your niece and you're giving her the benefit of a *balanced view*?'

'You're going down the wrong path,' says Sadie. 'I don't want to focus on Marie McShane.'

'Well, spit it out, then,' says Eddie, folding his arms.

'After talking to Marie, to Samantha, to Rosie, and after reading her diary, there's one person who's always been there. He went to Scarborough with the McShanes when Lila Foster was taken. He was seen close to the field where Lauren was found. He was in the area when Katie Masters disappeared. The only link that's missing is to Paige Lewis, who went missing when Rosie was in the secure unit. She was from Liverpool, but it was so long ago that I can't find a connection to him.'

'Who are you talking about?' I ask. 'Who was in all of these places?'

'A man called Mark Donovan,' says Sadie. 'He was a school friend of Rosie's brother Billy.'

'Do you know where he is now?'

'I don't know where he is for certain,' she says. 'But he's married to Rosie McShane. Last time I talked to her, she was living in the Gloucestershire area.'

'Oh God,' I say, falling back against my chair. 'So Rosie's married to a man who let her serve time in prison when he knew she was innocent?'

'I think so.'

'And not only that,' says Eddie, staring at the table. 'He's literally been getting away with murder ever since.'

'I find this all so hard to take in,' I say. 'If what you're saying is right, Sadie, then Rosie was telling the truth when she said she found Lauren lying in the field.'

'I don't know if I can believe all of this,' says Eddie, getting up to pace the kitchen. 'A jury found her guilty. The police were convinced it was her. Why would they lock her up if there was a chance she was innocent? Heck, you saw her with your own eyes, Heather.'

'This is all my fault,' I say. 'It was because Rosie didn't say anything – she didn't speak at all. She didn't seem upset. The poor child must've been in shock. Oh, God, what have I done?'

'I'm not having that,' says Eddie. 'You're not to go blaming yourself for anything. It's not your fault you found her. It's not as though you made it up.' He looks at Sadie. 'How can you be so sure it wasn't McShane?'

'The other girl, Paige Lewis, was found murdered weeks after she went missing. She had dried buttercups and daisies in her hair. It was the thirteenth of March 2001...'

'The same date...'

Eddie's shoulders slump.

'Lila, Lauren, Paige, Katie,' says Sadie, 'were all killed on the same day. Lila, Paige, and Katie weren't found straight away. But they all disappeared on the thirteenth.'

'Have you told the police?' Eddie asks, not looking up from the table.

'I've been in contact with the detective who took over Paige's case. Gave her all the information that I have.'

'So what do we do now?' Eddie asks. 'Go and talk to this Mark fella?'

'No,' she says. 'I don't want him to know we suspect him. I'm going to try to talk to Rosie – to the person she is today. She has a daughter now, too.'

'What?' Eddie's head shoots up. 'Oh. I see. Right. Yes, of course she has.'

I know the heartbreak he's feeling because I'm feeling it, too. Lauren should be living the same life as Rosie. Lauren should be sitting here with us, ordering Indian food. We could be picking our granddaughter up from school.

But we will never get that.

We can never have her back.

'Can I help you look through your research?' I say to Sadie. 'I might pick up on something you've not noticed.'

'If you're sure,' she says, passing me the notebook. 'This is Rosie's diary from 1992 to 1993. There's not much in there but you might find something that stands out, seeing as you were quite close and lived next door.'

'I'll try anything.' I pull it towards me, noticing the many hearts drawn in biro on the front of it. 'Eddie, load up the percolator. I think it's going to be a long night.'

'Why the thirteenth of March?' he says, still standing. 'What is so significant about that date?'

'I don't know, Ed,' says Sadie. 'That's something else I need to work out.'

'Do you think something happened in his childhood – did someone harm him on that specific date?'

'It's the eleventh today,' I say. 'Only two days away.'

'Jesus Christ,' says Eddie. 'How are we going to warn people? If he's roaming about trying to pick his next victim then we need to know if it's him for sure. Because I sure as hell won't just sit back and let it happen. We need to make sure we find him before another innocent child is murdered.'

CHAPTER 19

ROSIE MCSHANE'S DIARY

1st January 1992–13th March 1993

Rosie Alexandra McShane
Age: 9 (10 in 28 days, double figures!)
This is my new diary.
Keep OUT!!!!

<u>9 a.m.</u> My resolution is to keep writing in this diary so I can see at the end of this year how boring my life still is.

<u>8 p.m.</u> Today wasn't so bad, called for Lauren at half nine this morning like every day but then we went to the park and met a new girl called Samantha who says her dad's a policeman but me and Lauren reckon that's a lie. Samantha gave us 10p each, but there were no shops open to spend it so we buried it next to the tree with the love heart on it. Lauren said we should go back tomorrow and if the money is gone then we know that Samantha is a thief!!! Lauren says DON'T TRUST NEW PEOPLE.

But she might be being paranoid, like Uncle Davy is.

He thinks me and Billy steal from him ALL THE TIME.
P.S. We don't.

P.P.S. Am not just saying that in case Uncle Davy might read this. Or more likely Mum. I NEVER steal.

Can't say the same about Billy... YOU KNOW IT!!!

<u>*2nd January 1992*</u>

<u>*9 p.m.*</u> *Samantha's not a thief and Lauren was cross about it all day. Still no shops open to spend our 10p and it didn't multiply in the night like Lauren said it would. Who is the liar now, LAUREN!!!!*

P.S. Just kidding.

<u>*1st January 1993*</u>

Age: 10 almost 11

Right. This year I will <u>definitely</u> write more in here. I was too young to commit to anything last year. And no one ever found this diary so I think it's safe.

Things about me:

1 – Last year at primary school (sob!).

2 – I have a dog called Tilly that used to be my grandma's but she's dead now (Grandma not dog RIP).

3 – I am one hundred per cent in love with Ross Bradshaw who came over from actual America. He talks with an English accent, though, which was a bit of a let-down when the teachers bigged him up before he came but he is still the FITTEST BOY IN THE WORLD.

4– Lauren thinks the same, too. But we're not going to let him come between us. BFFs 4eva

5 – Ross doesn't actually know my name. He doesn't know Lauren's either, but it doesn't matter because we have face masks and matching hair bobbles from Chelsea Girl and we are going to go back to school after a makeover. Wish I had money for a new coat and some lip gloss (even Vaseline will do – can put it on eyelashes and eyebrows too, says Just Seventeen), but I need to make my personality SHINE instead.

PS. This is easier in theory than reality. I basically say nothing to no one except for Lauren. Must try new confidence strategies listed in *Nikki's* problem page. I shouldn't be still reading *Nikki* because it's made of comic paper and has comic strip stories, but hey. The old lady across the road gives me her granddaughter's old copies so I'm not actually buying them myself. And, like Mum always says, beggars can't be choosers. The problem page is the best bit of every magazine. Especially the ones in More! magazine that Lauren managed to steal from the doctor's. What was a magazine like that doing at the doctors?! Perverts.

9th March 1993

God I can't believe we used to like Ross Bradshaw. He turned out to be such a dick. What a cliché going for Rachel Mansfield as well. Idiot. Me and Lauren are well rid of that brain burden.

Can't believe Lauren's mum says she's not allowed to come to Scarborough with us!!!! Her mum said she wasn't allowed time off school and now Mum has said that Billy can take a friend instead and I'm going to be stuck in Yorkshire with him and his dickhead mate.

God. Kill me now. Will write to Lauren every day. Bet the caravan doesn't have a heater because Mum and Davy don't like spending ANY money on proper things. It's going to be FREEZING!

10th March 1993

11:13 p.m. *Been here one whole day and I have to sleep on the settee because the boys and my mum and Davy have the bedrooms. I might as well camp outside and freeze to death and then they'll be sorry. They're still not asleep yet (Mum and Davy) and they keep coming out their room to get bottles of beer from the fridge. God I hope they don't end up doing IT. They think I'm asleep. I can hear EVERYTHING in here. Kill me now.*

11th March 1993

8 a.m. *It's stupid that Billy and Mark are in the caravan with us because they're fifteen and well old enough to share a tent on their own but Mum says she doesn't have the cash to buy a tent so I'm the one who has to suffer. When I'm older I'm gonna have a job and be so rich and I'm never gonna be a parent. I'll have a caravan to myself and I'll wave at Mum and Billy and Davy from my window like the queen.*

P.S. Mum didn't appreciate me telling her all of that at ten to eight in the morning so I'm going for a walk to post Lauren's letter. Holidays are a big pile of crap.

6 p.m. *Finally I have a friend here! She's called Lila and she's nine months older than me. She's so pretty and she has a room in her caravan to herself because she doesn't have any brothers or sisters and I wish her parents would adopt me so we could be sisters. I will never tell Lauren any of this. It's bad enough that Lauren doesn't want me to be friends with Samantha any more. She likes it when it's just the two of us. I used to like that, too, but there are millions of people in this world. Just being friends with one of them can be pretty lonely when they're not there. I'm meeting Lila in twenty minutes and we're going to the pier to spend the money her parents gave us. How nice are they? They even put the coins in those little*

brown envelopes that the rich kids at school use to bring their
dinner money in. Her mum even drew a little rose next to my
name. I wish they'd invite me to stay over. Bet they have hot
chocolate before bed.

<u>10 p.m.</u> I hate my brother and his stupid friend. Why do they
have to spoil everything? Lila was my friend and they
wouldn't even let me have that. I'm so sorry, Lauren, for what
I wrote. You're my best friend in the whole world and you
always will be. You were right. DON'T TRUST NEW
PEOPLE!! I am so homesick right now I think I might die of
sadness.

<u>12th March</u>

<u>2 p.m.</u> Everything is OK. Lila didn't mean to leave me out last
night. She said that Mark kept talking to her and she didn't
want to be mean and tell him to get lost. It's hard telling older
boys to go away, especially when you don't know them, so I
understand. I can tell them both to get lost because I'm not
scared of them. They don't listen to me, they laugh, but they're
never proper mean to me. Probably because Davy slaps them
round the head if they give any cheek. Davy has been extra
nice to me since I started bringing him and Mum their beers at
night, every thirty minutes (this also makes sure they know I'm
awake). Anyway, today, me and Lila sat on the big grassy area
near the cliffs and she made me and her daisy chain head-
bands. It's the most beautiful thing anyone has ever given me.
I wish I could keep it forever but flowers always die. Depressing!! Wish I hadn't just learnt about analogies at school last
week. Or was it similes? Must try harder.

<u>10 p.m.</u> Ignore all the above. Lila was being nice to me to get to
my brother or Mark. I don't think she's decided yet. Snobby

cow! Thinks she's too good for me – like I'm the poor girl she's taken pity on. Well, she's in the same caravan park! She's welcome to them. She doesn't know how annoying and smelly they are. She'll have a shock when she finds out. God, I can't believe two fifteen year olds are hanging out with a twelve-year-old. Pair of idiots can't get a girl their own age. Embarrassing or what. Wait till I tell Lauren. She had a crush on Mark last year. Actually, maybe I won't tell her. Don't want to rub it in and hurt her feelings.

<u>Midnight</u> They think I'm asleep. I might not be as old as them, but I stayed up till three in the morning on Christmas Eve. Billy is hissing at Mark, telling him that he shouldn't have given Lila some Cinzano, and Billy is saying that she might die of alcohol poisoning and Mark is saying that's ridiculous – she puked most of it out. Mark says Billy's jealous because she got off with Mark. Billy thinks they should go and check to see if her mum opened the caravan door when they knocked and left her on the step before they ran away.

God, I hope she's OK. I know I said that she was a cow, but I don't want her to actually die. I'm not gonna sleep tonight for worry. I knew Mum shouldn't have invited those two. They'd have been less trouble at home setting the house on fire.

<u>13th March</u>

Lila is alive! We know because her parents came banging on the door at seven this morning asking if we knew who had given her booze last night and Davy said he had no idea, and almost kicked off, offended that Lila's dad had the cheek to come round here accusing him of trying to get a child drunk. He's not some kind of pervert, he said. They said sorry pretty quickly. Davy is over six foot and half as wide. No one messes with Davy. Mum slept through the whole thing, which isn't surprising because she never gets up in the morning and never eats breakfast. At least Lila's alive. Thank God we are leaving today, and of course the boys have gone AWOL when we're supposed to be packing. This has been the worst holiday I've ever had (the actual only holiday I've ever had – depressing). I'm definitely <u>never</u> gonna have kids and I'm definitely <u>never ever</u> staying in a caravan for as long as I live. When we grow up, me and Lauren will get our own flat. We've already started picking things out of the Argos catalogue. They have everything in the Argos catalogue.

CHAPTER 20

JESSIE

It's only quarter to eight in the evening, but I'm lying against the wall in a single bed next to Mia, who has finally gone to sleep. Thankfully, the curtains in Mum's spare room are dark but the room is still relatively light.

Mia takes a noisy breath and her eye lashes flutter, and I feel envious of her being fast asleep, of her innocence and her belief that everything in the world is harmless and joyful. I stroke her soft smooth cheek with my finger. Her lashes are so long, she looks like a sleeping angel.

I turn to lie on my back and face the ceiling. What might it be like to have parents who still live in the childhood home? When I was in Lancaster, before I had to flee, I met a woman – well, she was about the same age as me – twenty-one, twenty-two – called Kerry. She felt sorry for me that Christmas because I was going to spend the holiday alone in the shared house as Mum was going away with Billy. She invited me back to her parents' house and her bedroom was exactly how she left it before she went to university – the posters on the walls, polaroid photos Blu-tacked around her vanity mirror. Granted, she'd only been away for a few months, but some people don't know how lucky they are. Imagine having your parents still together – imagine having a father around. Someone who you could call on for advice or to help you move house.

I could never ask my mum things like that. It wouldn't occur to her that I would ever need her help, because she had to fend for herself from a young age. And didn't my brother and I know about it. *I started cooking when I was seven years old*, and, *My mother was never there for me*, and, *Except when she was dying and then I stayed at her bedside but she was so cross that she was leaving and she screamed about the unfairness of it all*.

I can't remember much about my grandmother, but watching someone who didn't want to die must've been awful. Billy used to talk about her a lot. I wonder if he witnessed her slow deterioration, too.

My phone lights up on the windowsill behind the curtain. But it's neither Mark nor Liza. Just spam from Domino's, informing me of their Monday night deal. Another life, right there. Mark and me on the sofa watching a film, eating pizza. Mark hates Mondays – he always likes to do something indulgent – even if it's just chilling in front of the telly with a glass of wine.

I select the text message thread between us. He still hasn't replied to the few texts I've sent to him since I've been here. It's not like him not to have asked if we got here OK, to say goodnight to Mia.

I can't contact Mark's mum to check on him; Judith is not good under pressure, no matter how stoic she thinks she is. Liza lives a bus ride away from our house, so it would be too much to ask her to go round. Perhaps if I offer to pay for her taxi she might, though. I text her to say I'm a little worried – as well as adding that I hope her job interview went well. I stare at it for ages and it remains unread. Are my messages getting through to anyone? I send a quick tester message to Mum to check my phone is actually working.

The front door to Mum's house, which is just a few feet from my head, opens.

'For fuck's sake,' hisses Mum. 'Oi!'

I slowly rise off the pillow and peek between the curtains. Mum's holding a cigarette and striding across the road towards a black Audi. She stops at the driver's side, takes a drag, and lobs the ciggie. She makes a circular motion with her hand, the universal signal to wind down the car window.

Jesus. What the hell is she doing?

This is why I moved away and why I seldom come back.

Mortifying.

She's shouting now yet I can't hear the words. An angry tirade.

Mia's sound asleep. There'll be no waking her, thank goodness. I double check the bedroom window is locked before shimmying down the bed, sliding off as quietly as I can. I take a last glance at her before closing the door.

I slip on my shoes by the front door, and walk out of the dark hallway, blinking in the daylight outside. Curtains are twitching in the house next door.

'Mum!' I look both ways before crossing the road. 'What's wrong?'

The low sun is reflecting on the car's windscreen, but as I get closer, I see there's a man at the steering wheel. He's in his late forties, early fifties, and his dark hair looks dyed; sunglasses rest on top of his head.

Mum takes out her mobile and takes his photo.

'Just admit it's you,' she says. 'You've been lingering outside my house since yesterday. And I saw you last week. Have you got something to do with these posts on the internet about my granddaughter?'

'It's just a coincidence that I'm here,' he says in an accent not local to here. 'I swear. And I've got nothing to do with your granddaughter.'

'Yeah, right,' says Mum. 'What's it about then? Has someone dobbed me in? I'm entitled to my benefits, you know. Mental health is a real struggle. I doubt you'll have any experience of that.' She sneeringly gazes the length of his car.

'You can't judge if a person has problems with mental health by the car they drive,' he says.

'He has a point, Mum,' I add. 'But why are we talking about this on the street?'

'He's been following me,' she says, 'and sending me threatening texts.'

'Can I have a look?'

She taps on to the Messages app and selects the texts in question. Both of them are dated today.

> SENDER UNKNOWN 18:45:
>
> I know you lied.

> SENDER UNKNOWN 19:20:
>
> People have died because of you.

'What are these about?' I say to Mum. 'They've probably got the wrong number. Have you tried ringing it?' I press the call button and hold it to my ear. 'It's ringing.'

Mum sticks her head through the man's car window.

'It must be on silent,' she says.

The man reaches into his suit pocket and takes out a phone. He holds it up to Mum.

'It's not me.'

'That proves nothing,' she says. 'Knowing you, you'll have more than one.'

I end the call and pass the phone back to Mum.

'You don't know me.' The man slides the phone back into his pocket. 'You're insane.'

'You can't say things like that,' says Mum.

He taps the side of his head as the window rises.

'Hey!' She bangs the window with a sleeve-covered fist. The car accelerates and I half-expect her to chase it down the street. I lightly take hold of her wrist in case, but she shakes my hand away. 'Do you believe that?' She holds up her phone and takes a photo of the car. 'That's the fourth one in as many weeks.'

'What?' I take a photo, too, then follow as Mum strides towards the house. 'Have you called the police? I'm going to send the number plate to Nicola.' I tap out the message as I walk. 'She said to make a note of anything out of the ordinary.'

Next door's front door opens. A man around the same age as I am steps out.

'The police won't be of any help,' says Mum. 'Oh, hello, Adam,' she says all sweetness and light. 'Sorry about all the fuss. I've been having some trouble with stalkers. They don't seem to leave me alone. It's like I'm famous or something.'

He laughs at her joke, but his eyes dart to me.

I shrug. He extends his hand.

'I'm Adam,' he says.

I shake his hand.

'I gathered.'

'This is Jessie,' says Mum. 'She's not always this rude. She's going through a bad time. Someone's posting online that her daughter has gone missing. It's always drama, drama.' She gives a tinkly laugh before opening the door and going inside.

My face is hot; my mouth drops open.

'It's not always drama,' I say to him. 'It's just a really strange time at the moment. Sorry... I...' I can't think of anything else to say. I put my head down, step inside and close the front door. 'Oh, God. He's going to think we're a couple of thugs.'

Mum kicks off her shoes. 'He can probably hear you if he's still standing outside. And you're hardly a thug, are you? You're wearing pink polka dot socks, for God's sake. Come on, let's get a brew. I feel invigorated. Women being strong – sticking up for ourselves.'

'Was it true what you said out there?' I speak in a quiet tone, hoping she'll get the hint and follow suit. I stop to peek round the bedroom door, where Mia's in the same position as I left her. 'About men stalking you? What does that person who sent the text messages think you lied about?'

'I'll bring the tea through,' she says. 'Stick the telly on, won't you? There's a new drama starting in a minute.'

I linger in the hall, watching as she breezily pops teabags into a teapot, and places cups on a tray. Nothing fazes that woman.

I wish I'd taken a photograph of the message Mark was sent from his so-called business associate. Perhaps Nicola could have traced the number, but I was too caught up in the panic that someone might reveal my true identity. My life now is so precarious – a house of cards that could come crashing down at any moment.

In the living room, I stay near the window. The man from next door is standing at the wall of their front garden, looking both ways. He turns round, and I'm too slow to move back from the window. Unthinking, I whip the curtains shut.

Great. Not only has he seen my mother screaming in the street, but he also probably thinks I'm extremely weird. I wish I had as thick a skin as she has.

'See what my evenings have turned into?' she says, placing the tray on a TV dinner table. 'I'll stick us some toast on later if you get peckish.'

I sit on the settee, and she sits in her chair that faces the telly, the remote on its arm. She switches on the TV and two women in suits are walking towards the end of a dark pier. I'll never be able to concentrate on anything this serious.

'Oh, I've missed the murder,' says Mum. 'It's not the same when I don't catch the beginning. Do you find that, too?'

'Um...'

'Don't tell me you don't watch *Lies and Deceit*?'

'It's on at Mia's bedtime, and we usually—'

'How long does it take to put her to bed?' She's leaning forward in her seat. 'You want to be careful with that.' She puts an ashtray on the table and lights up a cigarette. 'If you molly-coddle them now, you won't see them for dust when they're older.'

I stare at her for a few moments, waiting for her to let on that she's joking or that she's caught the irony of what she's said.

Nothing.

She leans over to the crammed sideboard and grabs a long wooden box. I'm relieved when it's only a stick of incense that she takes out. She lights it and places it into a small circular holder.

'Gets rid of the fag smoke,' she says. 'Mia won't smell a thing in the morning.' She leans back again and takes a long drag. 'Have you got a Netflix login we could use?'

'I thought you wanted to watch this.'

'Can't you remember it? You were never good at remembering the little things, were you?'

'What?'

She grabs the remote and selects the Netflix app.

'Can you ask your bloke what the details are?'

'Mark, you mean. I don't want to be bothering him about Netflix passwords. He's going through a horrible time at work!'

'Chill out, Jessie,' she says, shaking her head. 'It's only a bit of telly. You think he's sitting around at home? So what if you're watching something with your very own mother?' She rests her elbow on the arm of the chair. 'He's probably out at the pub – making the most out of being home alone.'

'Maybe that's why he hasn't been replying to me,' I say quietly. I reach out a hand. 'Give me the remote. I'll key in the details.'

'You're a love,' she says, standing over and reaching across. 'I haven't watched *Dead To Me* since our Billy was here and there's at least two more series on there. His bloody fiancée must've changed the password. How heartless is that? He'd set me up my own profile and everything.'

'That's an idea,' I say. 'I'll set one up in your name.'

'That's my girl. Don't want him to think you're sitting on your arse drinking tea. Ha. He probably doesn't know I've packed in the booze. He might think we're on a bender. But at least with us watching Netflix, he'll know we're having a quiet one.'

'As if we'd go on a bender with Mia in the house,' I say, but I doubt she remembers that she used to do it all the time. I key in her name and hand it over as she picks an avatar. 'I thought you got on with Billy's fiancée. You described her as Miss Perfect earlier.'

'Aha!' she says, smiling on one side of her face. 'There she is! I wondered when you'd find your spark. You've been like a shadow since you got here. You know I can get you some wine if you fancy it. Just because I'm not drinking, doesn't mean you can't.'

'I'm OK thanks, Mum.'

She's scrolling through programme after programme, but it's a blur to me.

'Are you going to tell me what's been going on with these people that have been watching you?' I ask. 'You told Adam next door you were being stalked.'

'I was exaggerating a bit,' she says, settling on an episode. 'It was a woman the first time. Like I told him, I thought they were from the DSS. You know, Universal Credit. Whatever they call it these days. You never know what people are like round here. I've only been here six months and they seem pretty snooty. The type to be jealous when they see someone in need getting what they deserve.'

'You mean benefits?'

'You're one to talk. Before Wonder Boy came back into your life, you weren't so well-off yourself. Or have you forgotten?'

'No,' I say, narrowing my eyes as the opening credits begin. 'I wasn't being judgemental. It wasn't called Universal Credit back then.'

'Sorry.'

'Anyway,' I say. 'How would they know how you pay for things?'

'It's not as though I'm going out to work every day, is it?'

'You could be working from home.' I look at her and I can tell she's not really concentrating on the programme, either. 'You haven't finished telling me about the messages you've been —'

She pauses the television.

'I didn't want to worry you, what with you coming so far with the little one, but I've been getting texts saying I've lied about something. That's why I thought it was someone benefit shaming me.'

I frown.

'But you haven't done anything. What do they mean? Do they mean back when you were drinking? Did you do something you can't remember?'

'Of course not.' She's narrowing her eyes again like she's trying to tell me something without talking. 'They've got me mixed up with someone else.' She gets up and sits next to me on the settee, taking hold of my hand, and it feels weird because I haven't held her hand for such a long time. 'You're not to worry. I'll not let anything bad happen to you or Mia.'

'Why would anything bad happen?'

'Well, we don't know much about your fella, do we? How do you know he hasn't sent someone up here? Perhaps he was lying about all that weird stuff with his business. Maybe he's decided that he wants full custody – that he wants to take Mia back home. Perhaps it was *him* who put up that Facebook post saying Mia was missing.'

She's so close I can smell her breath but there's no whiff of anything alcoholic. Perhaps she's on medication.

'You're not making s...' I start. *Choose better words, Jessie.* How can I say that she's flitting from one subject to another, inventing scenarios that couldn't possibly happen. That she has barely spent more than a few hours with Mark since he was fifteen, so how could she know what he is supposedly capable of? I take a deep breath in. 'Shall we talk about it tomorrow?' I say. 'Everything's getting jumbled in my mind.'

'Are you tired, is that what it is?' she says, placing her hand on my back. 'You've had a long day, especially with all that travelling. I haven't travelled longer than thirty minutes in years. Maybe we should go away to the seaside, me, you, and Mia. That'd be nice.'

I turn to face her. Her eyes are clear, hopeful. It's as though she means what she says. That she actually believes that us going away together would be a good idea.

'We've haven't had a holiday together since Scarborough.'

'Don't be silly,' she says, 'of course we have. Didn't I take you to Whitby the Christmas after you came out? You must remember that.'

'*You* went to Whitby,' I say, flatly, quietly. 'You took Billy and that bloke you were seeing. You said he paid for it all and you couldn't afford to add another room for me. I went to stay with my uni friend Kerry and her parents.'

'Really? Are you having me on? Did I really leave you out like that?'

I stretch my arms in front of me and open my mouth into what I hope looks like a yawn.

'I think I must be tired. When I'm tired I can't think straight. Sorry, Mum. I really appreciate you having us here. Shall I wash the cups before I turn in?'

'I'm only half way through my first cup.' She presses play on the TV. 'It's not even half past nine.'

'Sorry, Mum,' I say. 'I'll feel better tomorrow.'

'Good, good.' Her eyes are focussed on the television as I stand and head to the door. 'I thought we could go out tomorrow.'

'Where?' I smile to soften my words.

'The park, perhaps. Let Mia have a run about.'

'That'd be nice. Well, night. See you in the morning.'

'Goodnight, Jessie.'

The click of her lighter sounds as I close the living-room door.

* * *

Inside the bedroom, I try to unzip my case as quietly as I can. I always keep PJs on the top when travelling. Another sign that I am getting older and more sensible.

I check my phone for the hundredth time again today. There's still no reply from Mark. I try ringing him again, but this time it doesn't ring – it goes straight to voicemail, *What the hell, Mark?* Anything could've happened to Mia and me. Doesn't he care any more? Out of sight, out of mind?

My message to Liza hasn't been read, either. I know my phone is working – I saw my message on Mum's phone.

Mia sighs in her sleep. She's switched sides and is now facing the wall. Easier for me to slide into bed, but it's so small that I'm hovering on the edge. I know I'll be aching in the morning from staying in the same position all night.

My phone lights up; Liza's ringing me.

'Jessie!' she says. 'Thanks for your message. I got the job! Can you believe it?'

'That's amazing, Liza,' I say, sitting close to the bedroom door. 'Congratulations!'

'I just popped round to yours – sorry, I know it's late. You must've been putting Mia to bed.'

'I'm not at home.' I look at Mia again in case I'm disturbing her. 'I'm at my mum's – set off this afternoon. Didn't you get my message?'

'You're at your mum's? Gosh, sorry I just glanced over your message. In my own world. I'm so sorry, Jessie.'

'You don't have to be sorry,' I say. 'Someone's posted online that Mia's missing – we think it has something to do with one of Mark's business associates. Threatening us, that type of thing.'

'Oh my god, Jessie, that's awful. Have you told the police?'

'I have a contact... I mean, yes. I've told the police. The posts have been taken down. I can't find them any more. I wish I'd taken a screenshot of them, but we saw them on Mark's laptop. My head was a mess.'

'I'm not surprised, Jessie. That's so weird. Really creepy. Do you want me to come up there for moral support? I can get a train first thing.'

'It's OK. The police are aware and my mum's here. She's not afraid of much, to be honest.' I hear the whoosh of what sounds like a bus going past. 'Are you outside? Is that traffic?'

'Like I said – I popped round to yours. I'm waiting at the bus stop.'

'Was there anyone in?' I feel my heart pounding. 'Did you see Mark?'

'No one answered the door. I thought you both might've been hiding from me after the other night. I felt really bad about that.'

'A lot's happened since then. Just forget about it. Was Mark's car outside the house?'

'Yes. The curtains were open and the lights were on. I thought I saw someone ducking behind the sofa, but Mark wouldn't do that, would he?'

'It depends on who he thought was at the door.' I cringe – I hope she doesn't take that the wrong way. 'I think something's wrong, Liza,' I add quickly. 'He hasn't answered my texts or phone calls. I've even tried the landline and there's no answer. It's just not like him. At the very least, he'd be checking to see if Mia's all right.'

'It does sound odd.' There's a hint of something in her voice but I can't tell what it is. 'Do you think he's seeing someone else?' she says. 'That all of this was a way to get you and Mia out of the house?'

'You're the second person to say that.' I'm dying to stand and pace the floor; my legs are starting to cramp. 'My mum suggested Mark was the one posting to social media, but he was as shocked as I was. There's something going on here. Mark wouldn't want to hurt Mia or me.'

'It was just a thought,' she says, sounding hurt. 'It was just the most likely explanation compared to some business mafia dudes coming round to beat him up.'

'You don't think they have, do you?'

'I was just kidding. Sorry – it was a bad time to joke. Sorry, Jessie.' A hydraulic hiss sounds in the background. 'My bus is here. Shall I get on or do you want me to check the house again?'

'No, no,' I say. 'You get your bus. If something's happened then I don't want you getting hurt trying to find out.'

'You really think it's that serious?' She pauses to say thank you to the bus driver. 'He's probably gone for a night out with friends. Or perhaps he's just popped to the shop. It seems a bit of a reach to think someone's broken in and kidnapped him or something.'

'Yes. You're probably right. Thanks, Liza. He probably hasn't realised his phone's out of charge. Or he might've dropped it in the loo again.' I laugh lightly. 'That'll probably be it.'

'If you need me to pop round tomorrow,' she says, 'it'll be no bother. I don't start my new job until next Monday.'

'Thanks, Liza. If I don't hear from him by lunchtime, I'll pay for a taxi for you. I don't want you out of pocket because my husband's being so lax with his phone.'

'I like to be useful, Jessie.'

'Thank you. And well done again on the job. I'm so glad you've finally found something. Though, I'll miss you popping into the studio.'

'So will I.'

The idea of being back at my studio, radio on, and losing myself in my painting is such a world away right now.

We say our goodbyes, and I stare at the unread messages to Mark, willing them to change to *read*.

A sound of a cup falling onto the floor sounds from the hallway.

'Sorry, sorry,' Mum hisses.

These walls are thin. She must've been listening at the door, though she can't have heard much; my voice was quiet. I move my head closer to the door. She's in the kitchen, now, tap on.

Sober, or not, Mum's behaviour is really odd.

I stare at Mark's contact photo on my phone.

She's not the only one.

CHAPTER 21

SADIE

9th August 2003

Sadie Harrison – Investigative Journalist

Interview with Sylvia Rossetti – grandmother of Samantha

Location: 3 Grafton Street, Clayton

Time: 17:15

Sadie Harrison (SH): Thank you so much for talking to me.

Sylvia Rossetti (Sylvia): Don't see that it's going to be much use, but anything to help.

SH: Do you remember hearing the news that Lauren Jones was murdered?

Sylvia: Of course. It was Mother's Day. My daughter came up with the kids.

SH: So it's not just Samantha?

Sylvia: No, she has two brothers. Right little tearaways, they were. Samantha's the eldest. She used to love going out to play with those two girls. I made them some orange cordial one day, gave them a plate of biscuits so they could have a little picnic in the garden.

SH: What did you make of Rosie McShane?

Sylvia: I didn't talk to her much. She looked as though she never brushed her hair, poor thing.

SH: Poor thing?

Sylvia: I know what they said about all of that, but can you see a little girl like that killing another? It'd take strength to hold her hands over the mouth like that.

SH: They were found together.

Sylvia: That doesn't mean much, does it?

SH: What time did Samantha come back from playing with Lauren and Rosie?

Sylvia: About ten minutes before I heard the sirens. She came back crying and screaming. I thought the sirens were the police for Samantha.

SH: What? Why was she so upset?

Sylvia: Upset? She was distraught. She said she was playing hide and seek with the girls – she couldn't find either of them. She said she was wandering round the forest on her own – well, it seems like a forest when you're twelve years old.

SH: She was distraught because she got lost?

Sylvia: No, no. She said a boy came up to her... he offered some of his juice... She started to feel woozy, so he guided her into this makeshift den.

SH: What? Did you tell the police about this?

Sylvia: Nothing happened to her. Rosie was hiding in the den. The boy ran off.

SH: Did Samantha know who this boy was? Did Rosie know him?

Sylvia: Samantha said he was tall with dark hair, but she didn't know his name. When we gave the description to the police, they didn't know either. They just saw it as kids' play. It was a different time, then. They had a dead girl to contend with.

SH: And they didn't make a connection between the two incidents?

Sylvia: They might've done. I don't know. But they never came back to the house to talk to us.

SH: Did you ever hear from the police again?

Sylvia: No. Samantha had been in trouble before, you see. Nothing big, just silly kids' stuff – pinching some sweets from the corner shop. The police thought Sam was making it up about being with Rosie – they'd already branded her a liar. And they thought they had Lauren's murder neatly solved – especially with Heather catching Rosie 'red handed'. The police didn't believe Samantha because they said Rosie couldn't be in two places at one time. It's an awful thing, isn't it? The community was never the same again. No children playing in the street – well, not for a good few years. There were some who never believed Rosie did it, but the police were convinced.

SH: As were a jury.

Sylvia: So why the questions? What are you trying to find?

SH: I'm trying to build up a picture of what went on that day. Did Samantha say anything about them picking flowers?

Sylvia: Lord, no. Samantha wasn't one for picking flowers and all of that. You'd more likely find her kicking a football around with the lads.

SH: Where is she now – Samantha?

Sylvia: Her and her parents moved to Canada. Thought it was a safer way of life. I haven't seen them in a few years. I'm too old to travel. My son set me up with a computer that has a camera.

SH: That's nice.

Sylvia: It's not as good as having them in the same country. They're coming to see me next year, though. I tell you. After what happened with that young girl, for a lot of people, nothing was the same again.

CHAPTER 22

JESSIE

Tuesday, 12th March

I forget where I am when I wake. My shoulders sink into the pillow, when it hits me that I'm at my mother's house. I dreamt about her last night. I was in a darkened room behind bars – which didn't actually happen at the secure unit – and she had the keys. She dangled them in front of me, laughing, before walking slowly away. It's one I've had at least five times over the past twenty years.

I sit up quickly.

Mia's not here.

I throw the covers off, dash to the door, and run to the living room.

No sign of her there.

The smell of cigarette smoke comes from the kitchen.

Mum's standing at the back door.

'Where's Mia?' I grip either side of the door surround. 'I did bring her with me, didn't I?'

'Morning to you, too,' she says, breathing smoke from her

lungs into the once-fresh air. ''Course you brought her with you. Are you having an episode again?'

'I don't have episodes, Mum. Where is she?'

'She's in my room,' she says, grinding the ciggie into an ashtray next to her on the kitchen counter. 'She was crying in the night and there was no waking you so I brought her in with me. You needed your sleep; you were exhausted last night.'

I go to Mum's bedroom door, closing my eyes for a second. *Please let Mia be OK.* I push it open. She's curled up on the top left corner of the double bed, pillows surrounding her like a nest.

I can't see her breathing. Oh God, let her be all right.

She takes in a deep breath and sighs, and I collapse to the floor.

'Jessie,' Mum hisses at the door. 'What the hell's wrong with you? Do you think I'd harm her? My own grandchild?'

Mia turns over and slowly opens her eyes. I almost dive next to her.

'Are you OK, my love?' I say, stroking her hair.

She nods, rubbing her eyes.

'Marie came to me when I was crying,' she says, shuffling herself up. 'Why didn't you wake up, Mummy?'

'I don't know. It's not like me at all. I'm so sorry, honey.'

'It's all right, Mummy.' She crawls to the side of the bed and slides off. 'Marie gave me some midnight toast.'

'You tried marmalade, too, didn't you, Mia?' says Mum.

Mia looks at me sincerely.

'I didn't like the marmalade, Mummy. It made me do this.'

She puckers her lips and squeezes her eyes shut.

'Shall we get you some breakfast, then?' says Mum. 'I think I might have some Shreddies somewhere.'

I'm still sitting on the bed as I watch my mother take my daughter by the hand and lead her out the room. It's often the case that some people make better grandparents than parents. Mum was only sixteen when she had my brother, and twenty when she had me.

I haven't been in her room before now. The bed has a plush pink headboard that clashes with the yellow woodchip wallpaper. There's a dark pine wardrobe against the back wall and a matching set of drawers opposite.

I stand and take a peek inside her wardrobe. It's only a third full, with creased jumpers and shirts on wire coat hangers, and three pairs of jeans folded at the bottom. Tears come to my eyes. I should've been helping her more – should've visited more often. But I didn't know she'd stopped drinking. She could be so vile when she was drunk and she would never remember in the morning, never knowing what I wanted her to be sorry for.

I close the wardrobe doors gently; I'm invading her privacy. She wouldn't want me to see her pathetic array of clothes. I feel a pang of guilt that I never used to feel when I had bad thoughts about her. She's changed. I should stop treating her as though she's the same person she used to be.

Mia stands at the door cradling a bowl in her little hands.

'Marie asks if you want some cereal.'

'It's OK,' I say, leaving the room, and watching her as she carries the swishing cereal slowly towards the living room. 'Try not to spill that.'

'I'm not trying to spill it, Mummy,' she says haughtily.

'Do you want me to put the television on for you?' I ask.

'It's already on *CBeebies*.' Mia places the bowl on the coffee table and kneels on the floor. 'I put it on while Marie made my cereal.'

'Right,' I say. 'Very good.'

I don't want to be here any more. Why isn't Mark answering my calls? Hopefully Liza will text me soon, tell me that Mark's home, and everything's OK. It was just a misunderstanding. Then Mia and I can go home, get her back into school, and we can carry on and forget about this. Just a blip. I'm lucky that nothing has happened for years. It was just some idle threat from someone who doesn't know my background. Or perhaps Mark let it slip to them. Perhaps he got drunk with them during one of his boozy dinners he schmoozes his clients with. Maybe he wanted to impress them and now it's backfired.

Whatever it is, he'll sort it. He always comes to my rescue. He's just making sure it's safe for us to come back. I hope he doesn't do anything silly and get himself into trouble.

'Jessie!' shouts Mum. 'Come and get your breakfast.'

I walk to the kitchen with a sense of dread. Not at what she's prepared for me, but the feeling in the pit of my stomach. Liza said the lights were on at our house, and it looked as though someone was in our house. Coupled with the threats to my daughter, and the man waiting outside Mum's in his car... I should be more worried, shouldn't I?

'I think we should leave,' I say, because I can never keep things inside. Mum always said I was too honest. As if it were a bad thing. 'I panicked when I woke. I thought someone had taken her.'

'No you didn't.' She doesn't look up from buttering a slice of toast. 'You thought I'd done something to her, didn't you? The way you looked at me before. It's like you really hate me sometimes.'

'I don't hate you, Mum.'

'I tried my best, you know. It's hard to show affection when I never grew up with it.'

She's been saying that for years: *I tried my best*. As if merely acknowledging it redeems her from the years when she barely gave Billy and me any attention.

I distract myself by focusing on the fridge magnet again. The photo of Billy and his wife-to-be that I haven't even met.

'Did I ever tell you,' Mum asks, standing next to me, 'that

my mother had me and my brother while she was taking the contraceptive pill? I mean, she probably didn't take it properly because it was new, back then. Two pregnancies over three years, and neither of us were actually wanted. It'd be funny, now, I guess. If she were still alive we might have joked about it.'

'That's horrible,' I say. She hands me a plate of toast, and another plate that rattles with two egg cups on it: one filled with marmalade, the other with jam. It's a gesture that makes my eyes fill with tears. 'Why did she tell you that?'

Mum shrugs, takes another ciggie out the packet and opens the back door.

'Do you want me to make you a coffee?' I ask her, placing my plates on the side. I flick on the kettle, then rinse her empty cup, even though she hasn't replied. 'Do you think about it a lot? What your mum said?'

The kettle boils and I pour water into the cup of instant granules, top it with an inch of cold water and hand it to my mum.

'Yes,' she says. 'More often now than before. I guess that's what happens when you're sober. Everything is more vivid. Sometimes it's as though it's just happened.'

She sways slightly and grabs hold of the backdoor handle.

'Why don't you sit on that plastic chair?' I say. 'To save you standing at the back door all the time.'

She laughs wheezily, then coughs for a full thirty seconds.

She stands, recovered.

'I don't always stand *here* having a fag, do I?' She wipes her eyes with the sleeve of her cardigan. 'It's because you two are here. I normally watch Susannah and whoever she has on with her in the mornings, don't I? My favourite of the other ones is Ben Shephard. Proper nice, he is. No skeletons there. The days roll into one for me, though. Morning television helps me realise what day it is.'

'Sorry, Mum.'

'I didn't say that to make you feel bad, Jessie.' She takes a sip of her coffee. 'That's perfect, that is. Hey, do you fancy going for that walk later? They've just kitted out the children's park. It's lovely, surrounded by trees. There's a pond, too. Mia will like that.'

'I'd like that, too,' I say. 'Are you OK to watch Mia while I get washed and dressed?'

'Of course!' She says it with a smile. 'I've put some fresh towels in the bathroom.' She places the still-full mug on the side as she closes and locks the back door. 'I'm getting quite used to having company. I think I like it.'

'Thanks, Mum.' I check the living room, where Mia is sipping the milk from the bowl. 'Just going to get ready, Mia. Won't be long.'

'OK, Mummy.'

* * *

The bathroom's white and very clean with a faint smell of bleach. On a bamboo shelving unit are rolled-up towels and a selection of toiletries. Some, I note, are labelled 'For Men'. Mum's not had a total personality transplant, then.

I turn the dial on the shower and am about to undress when my mobile rings.

'Hey, Liza.'

I flick off the noisy, clanging shower.

'Hi, Jess,' she says. 'I hope I'm not interrupting you.'

I move my phone from my ear to check the time. It's half past nine already.

'No, no. I've not long got up, to be honest. It's not like me at all.'

'Have you heard from Mark since last night?' she asks. 'Only, I'm outside your house and the curtains are closed. So that must mean he's been here, mustn't it?'

'Oh, thank God.' I sit down on the edge of the bath. 'I wonder why he hasn't called, though.'

'Have you tried his office?'

'His assistant said he booked yesterday off. Are the cameras still working?' I ask. 'Can you tell from there? I wish I had the app on my phone.'

'I don't know. Is there meant to be a light shining from it?'

'I don't know either.'

'I have a really strange feeling about this,' she says, voicing my own fears. 'I've rang the doorbell loads of times and climbed over the back gate. One of your neighbours came out and said there was another man here last night. Pulled up in a black Mercedes or something. I think he thought I was robbing the place. What if Marks's slipped and fallen? What if that man last night attacked him?'

'But you said last night not to worry – that he's probably out with friends or something. Perhaps he drank too much that he's sleeping it off. It's still early if he came back late last night.'

'I was trying to calm you down last night,' she says. 'But I think there might be something wrong. Did he say he had plans to travel anywhere?'

'No. Do you think I should call the police?'

'I don't know. Sorry, Jess. I'm not being much help, am I? I think you might have to ring his family – see if they've heard from him. He might be staying with his parents – especially if he thinks someone's looking for him.'

'I think you're right. That must be it. Thanks so much for your help, Liza.'

'Any time.' She hesitates and then asks me: 'Do you have a spare key anywhere? Or do you want me to break in?'

'What?' I'm taken aback. 'No to both. But thanks. Bye, Liza.'

'Goodbye, Jessie.'

I don't know if it's my imagination running away with me,

but that phone call has shaken me. Not just that Mark's not answering, but that the curtains have been drawn and a man was seen outside. And Liza thought nothing of breaking into my house. What if she's done that before?

CHAPTER 23

Help Find Mia Donovan

Today 11.23 (Admin scheduled)

This is a photo of Mia Donovan who is only four years old and has been missing from home since this morning. Please share. We believe she is in imminent danger.

Elaine Dickinson: *Shared Devon. Hope she's found soon*

DaveThom: *Shared Blackpool*

TerriMae: *poor wee thing so cute.........shared Birmingham*

Ash Singh: *Shared Leeds*

Melanie Jane: *Shared Manchester. Praying for your safe return little one*

Leon Wolfe: *Is this legit?*

View more comments.

CHAPTER 24

JESSIE

Mum has packed a tinfoil package of jam sandwiches, and Mia's carrying them in a picnic basket that looks almost half the size of her. The basket was already in one of the cupboards when she moved in, apparently; it is not something my mother would buy. I don't think she's been on a picnic in her life.

'Isn't this lovely,' says Mum, eyes closed and face towards the sun. 'I don't go for walks often enough.'

'It is.'

'What's wrong?' she asks. 'You sound so maudlin'. Are you still on edge, thinking something's happened to Mark or that he might come and steal Mia?'

She says it so lightly – why doesn't she think about what she's saying?

'Liza says she hasn't seen him. She said there was a man at the house last night. But she didn't actually see *him* either; it was one of our neighbours who mentioned it to her. I couldn't tell you before because Mia might've heard.'

'A man at the house?' Mum stops and rests a hand on my arm. 'Sounds like they could be casing your joint. Hope you don't display all your expensive gadgets near the windows.'

'Liza said that yesterday all the lights were on and she could've sworn someone was inside. And this morning, all lights are off and the curtains are closed.'

'Sounds like Mark's trying to avoid her.' She starts to walk again because Mia's getting further from us.

'I need to ring Judith,' I say, 'to see if he's there. Let's give Mia a nice morning, then I'll give her a ring.' I quicken my pace so we're right behind her. 'If they've not heard anything then I'll phone the police. Do you think we should be out here in the open like this? What if it's not a prank and someone's really after Mia?'

'We'll keep a close eye on her, but it'll be a mistake. Wires crossed or something.'

'Have you received any more texts?'

'I get them all the time, but I'm used to them. Ignore and block. It won't have anything to do with you and Mark.'

'If you get any more, don't delete them. Just in case.'

Mia has spotted a woman sitting on a bench with a puppy on her lap. She speeds up towards her.

'Mia!' I shout. 'Wait for us. Don't talk to strangers, remember.'

'At least it's busy here with families,' says Mum.

We round a bend and there's a fenced play area with about thirty children playing on swings, climbing frames, and metal animals on giant springs. Mia turns and runs back towards me as fast as she can, carrying that huge basket.

'Please can you look after my lunch, Mummy,' she says. 'I need to get on that elephant when it's empty.'

I take the basket and open the gate for her, and she runs towards the animal.

Mum lingers, taking a ciggie out the packet.

'You go ahead,' she says. 'I'll have this and I'll come in when I've finished.' She nods to a group of women sitting at a wooden picnic table, in a uniform of waterproof jackets and white trainers that look as though they've never touched mud. 'Don't want the parenting police on my case.'

I sit on the one spare wooden bench and watch Mia. She gives up on the elephant and heads towards the small slide. She stands aside to let a younger child go up the stairs first. She's so kind to younger kids.

'Is it OK if I sit here?'

I look up and the woman in front of me is a shadow against the sun. I take off my sunglasses.

'Sure.'

The woman sits. She's about the same age as me, with dark curly hair. She's also wearing one of those jackets, Boden or wherever they buy their quilted gilets. They must give them out on maternity wards around here.

'I like your jacket,' I say.

'Thanks.' She brushes off dust that's not there. 'Got it from one of the charity shops on the high street.' She leans closer. 'They're a bit posher round here.' She glances at the group. 'I always worry someone's going to recognise their old clothes and stop me on the street, but it hasn't happened yet.' She holds out a hand. 'I'm Melanie.'

'I'm Jessie.'

'That's such a lovely name,' she says. 'Which one's yours?'

'The little girl in the yellow coat. I always buy her bright jackets so I can pick her out in a park, but it seems everyone here had the same thought.'

'Cute.' She reaches into her coat and pulls out a pair of sunglasses and puts them on. 'There's nowhere for them to get lost in this little bit. It's by the pond that you want to be careful.'

A slight breeze wafts from the right; it makes me shiver.

'Guess you forgot your own jacket?' she says.

'Which child is yours?' I ask.

She lifts up her glasses, sliding them onto her head like a headband.

'The one who's sitting on the ground pulling out grass and eating it. Oh, God.' She gets up and runs over to the little boy who now has mud around his mouth. She takes him by the hand and guides him to the bench and plonks him down. She kneels before him and takes out a pack of wet wipes from her large bag next to the bench. She plucks one out and cleans the boy's face. 'I don't know, Del. What are we going to do with you?'

Face clean, she puts him back on the ground and he walks to the mini slide.

'Del?' I say. 'That's an unusual name for a child, these days.'

'It's a family name.'

'Oh.'

'He suits it, actually,' she says, with good humour. 'I haven't seen you here before. Have you just moved to the area?'

'No.' I glance towards the fence. Mum is on her second cigarette; the thought of being unable to smoke for ten whole minutes has obviously sent her into panic mode. 'I'm staying with my parents.'

'Nice.'

It's easier to say *parents*. No one questions *parents*. If it were *mum* there'd be a whole narrative that I'd have to explain. And it's not as though I'm going to see this woman again.

'Have you lived round here long?' I ask.

'A few years,' she replies, shielding her eyes, searching frantically then relaxing as she spots her little boy again.

'Mummy,' shouts Mia from the top of the slide. 'Is it time for jam sandwiches yet?'

'Soon,' I yell back.

Mel frowns.

'Is that your daughter?'

She's taking out her phone.

'Yes, why?'

'I saw a post this morning.' She scrolls through the Facebook app. 'About a missing child. I shared it to my page. Here.'

She hands me her phone, and there is a picture of Mia.

It's been shared all over the country by strangers.

'But my daughter's not missing.'

She shuffles slightly away, frowning as she stares at me.

'She's definitely my daughter.' I scramble into my pocket for my purse. 'Here. My driving licence. Same surname. And look at my phone. Pictures of Mia through the years.'

'What's going on,' Mum asks. 'Is everything OK?'

Mel's staring, unblinking, at Mum. She holds the phone up to her.

'That's the same post I saw,' says Mum. 'The exact same but dated a few days ago.'

'But why would someone do that if she isn't missing?'

This woman doesn't trust us at all, I know it.

'I've no idea. Someone playing a sick joke.' I stand. 'Come on, Mia. It's time for your picnic.'

Mia comes running over. Mel reaches over to her, but I swipe her arm away.

'Hey, Mia,' she says. 'Is this really your mummy?'

Mia scrunches her nose, moving closer to me, hiding behind my legs.

'Mummy, why is that lady looking at me like that?'

Mel stands.

'I'm so sorry,' she says. 'I've heard that men, women, sometimes do that to locate their children. Abusive exes. Things like that. I'll report the post. OK?'

'Come on, you two,' says Mum, walking towards the gate. 'We need to get out of here.'

'Mum,' I say quietly when we reach the path. 'In that photo, Mia's wearing the clothes she has on now. And her hair is in a ponytail, just like it is today.'

'Shit.' She turns around, looking for anyone who might be watching us. 'We need to go to the police. Right now.'

CHAPTER 25

HEATHER

We stayed up until three this morning, poring over documents Sadie had transcribed from her various interviews, and now I'm sitting at the kitchen table with yet another coffee, waiting for Sadie to get up. She doesn't half like her lie-ins. Some things never change. Eddie got up at seven as usual. He's taking his constitutional walk, getting a paper, and probably sneaking in a crafty cigarette after 'giving up' twenty years ago.

After he went to bed at midnight, Sadie played me one of Rosie's tapes. Hearing her young voice was like being transported back in time. *They said my house is like a shell*, she said. That's what I keep replaying in my mind. I didn't visit their house often. We weren't friends like that, Marie and me. I'd have lent her teabags, or some sugar or flour if she asked but she never did. I used to see Rosie, sometimes Billy, doing the shopping. Once I saw her hand a note over to Mrs Alderton at the corner shop, saying she had Marie's permission to buy twenty Bensons. The things we got our children to do in disguise of their freedom. The kids playing out suited the parents. Sometimes they even skipped lunch. I'd leave Lauren a sandwich in the fridge that she'd pick up without me noticing.

Was Rosie's house like a shell inside? I called round once to drop some letters that had come to ours by mistake, and I couldn't help peeking inside. It wasn't often they had the living-room curtains open. The floors weren't carpeted and I couldn't tell if it was meant to be like that or not because sanded floor-boards were just becoming a bit of a trend. There were two mismatched settees and a rag rug under the gas fire. It wasn't messy or anything. Just didn't have the same amount of clutter I used to have. Every surface used to be covered at our house: miniature ceramic cottages, brass fire accessories, even though we had a gas fire, too. Got rid of all of that when we moved. Sold most of the furniture, as well. I wanted to start afresh, even if it was in the same town. I kept most of Lauren's things, though. I still have a few things dotted around the place, but it's still too painful to look at her clothes, her toys, her books.

It's almost half eleven when Sadie wanders into the kitchen. She's wearing jeans and a huge jumper that almost reaches her knees.

'Didn't think about the weather when I packed yesterday,' she says.

'I don't know why someone as intelligent as you thinks reading the weather forecast's beneath you,' I say, getting up to make her a cup of tea.

'It's not beneath me, Heather.' She sits at the table. 'I just forget. My mind's always busy with other things.'

'I suppose if I had your brain' – I pour hot water onto a bag of English Breakfast Tea – 'I'd be too busy to worry about the rain, too.'

'Stop putting yourself down.' She gets up to get the sugar because I always forget. 'You're still only young – fifty's the new forty.'

'Give over. I'm almost halfway through my sixties already.'

'The glass is still half full, Heather,' she says, stirring the spoon like she's ringing a bell.

'So,' I say as we sit at the same time, 'what's our plan of action?'

'I need to speak to Rosie,' she says. 'But first I have to find her. I haven't talked to her for over four years – she didn't give me her most recent address. It's not as though I can just look her up online. I always had to wait until she contacted me when she moved somewhere new.

'I've employed a few of my contacts and they're working on it. Have to keep it quiet, though. I couldn't tell them who they were actually looking for – not her old identity. I don't want them getting into trouble with the police. They take lifelong anonymity extremely seriously. I haven't seen her for so long. I feel as though I'm letting her down by not finding the real killer.'

'You haven't let her down,' I say. 'You've never given up looking.' I drop my gaze. 'Unlike me.'

'You should stop beating yourself up about everything, Heather. It was out of your control. You weren't to know.' She's scrolling through her phone. 'One of my mates has emailed. He says there's a Mark Donovan originally from Manchester who's now living in Cheltenham with his wife and daughter.'

'Do you think that's the same one?'

'I'm not sure. I have to be careful,' she says. 'There are still loads of people online – and from Clayton – who wonder what Rosie looks like today. Some have even posted pictures of other women who had the same dark hair and big brown eyes. They'd have got prison time if they'd shared a real photo of Rosie as she is now.'

'If we can't find her,' I say, 'we can always ask Marie. Eddie said he saw her last year. She was standing in line at the post office in town. She didn't see him, though. He said she kept her head down.'

'Marie would never tell us where Rosie is.' Sadie's frowning at her phone. 'Hey. Look at this.'

She slides it towards me.

'It's a Facebook post,' she says, 'saying that a Mia Donovan is missing from this area. Do you think it's a coincidence that Mark's surname is Donovan? Rosie's daughter must be around the same age now, wouldn't she? About four years old?'

I pass the phone back.

'I have no idea. I didn't know you kept in contact with her, remember? I only found out yesterday.'

'The little girl has the same dark hair as Rosie,' she says. 'She's the spitting image of her. Put the radio on, Heather. There might be something on the news about her.'

We listen to the five minutes of headlines on the local news station, but nothing mentions a missing child.

'That's so strange,' I say. 'When was the post created?'

'Monday, then another this morning. The same post is repeated – and it's sponsored. That's so odd. But that would mean the posts are traceable. They'd have to give their card details to process the payment.' She slides her finger across the screen. 'Someone has tagged a Mark Donovan, asking if this is true. Must be one of his friends. His profile is extremely private, though. There isn't even a profile photo.'

The front door opens and closes.

Eddie puts the car keys on the hall table and comes straight into the kitchen.

'You'll never guess who's back,' he says, lingering by the door.

'Rosie McShane,' says Sadie, still looking at her phone.

'What?' he says. 'How the heck do you know that? Was it in the news? She's not meant to be round here, is she?'

'I don't know about that,' says Sadie, 'but we think her daughter Mia is in the news. Where did you see her? Were there reporters there – the police?'

'No,' he says. 'Why would there be? Has she done something wrong?'

Sadie passes Eddie her phone.

'This doesn't make sense,' he says. 'I was going to tell you that I've just seen Rosie and her mum in the park. They had a little girl with them. She was wearing the exact same outfit as this.' He passes Sadie's phone back and takes his out of his pocket. 'I took a photo of them.' He holds it up for us to see. 'Look.'

'Eddie!' I say. 'You can't go round taking pictures of kids. What if they think it's you who posted this? You'd better delete it before anyone catches you.'

'Who's going to catch me?' he asks. 'Big Brother doesn't track what people do on their phones. Not officially.'

He slides his phone back into his pocket as the landline on the wall next to him starts to ring.

Sadie almost jumps out of her skin.

'I can't believe you still have a landline, Heather,' she says.

'It's for you,' says Eddie. 'It's The Haven.'

As I stand, I find my stomach sinking.

I glance at Sadie and feelings of dread and doom pass between us.

'Heather Jones,' says the lady at the other end. 'I'm calling to let you know that your mum had a small heart attack this morning.'

'Oh God,' I gasp out, shocked. 'Is she still alive?'

'Yes, yes,' she replies. 'Sorry. I was meant to say that first. But we don't know how long she'll still be with us.'

'I'm coming,' I say. 'We're coming right away.'

I turn around to see Sadie standing.

'Shall I wait...?' Eddie starts.

'Don't worry, Ed,' I say. 'You stay here. We don't want too many people in Mum's room.'

'Right you are,' he says, a little relieved. He only lost his own mother last year. He visited her every day for three months and it took its toll on him. 'Let me know if you need anything. I can pop to the shops if you're there a while.'

'Thanks, love.' I give him a hug before heading to the hall for my coat.

Sadie opens the front door and we rush down the path and get into her car.

* * *

We drive in silence for the first couple of minutes. I can't stop thinking of my lovely mum lying there on her own in that room. What if we're too late? I hope she knows I love her. I only saw her the day before yesterday, but now it seems like months ago. It's awful how our bodies can let us down so quickly.

Sadie's frowning.

'We'll make it,' I say, wishful thinking. 'She'll hang on for us.'

She nods slowly. She's probably not even thinking about Mum.

'Why would someone do that?' she asks. 'Put a post up, saying her daughter's missing?'

'It's probably some sick joke,' I say, looking out the window.

'But why though?' Sadie presses. 'Rosie's served her time. If they've leaked Mia's identity, they'll be in massive trouble. They could get prison time themselves.'

'What about Paige's mother, Kathleen?' I say. 'We only saw her yesterday – we said the murders might be connected – and now someone's threatening to take Rosie's daughter.'

'But I told her I knew it wasn't Rosie – there's no way she could have confused my words. Do you think whoever it is, is threatening to take Mia? Or is it a warning? Rosie must know about this, and that's why she's come home. Everyone knows who she is around here. She's not hiding in plain sight any more.

If anything were to happen, the whole town would know about it.'

'It does sound plausible. She'll have told her liaison at the police or courts or whoever it is. It looks like someone's trying to compromise her new identity.'

Sadie indicates left into the car park.

'Here we are.'

'Let's not talk about this any more,' I say. 'Please. Let's just be here for Mum.'

Sadie turns off the ignition.

'Of course.' She reaches over and takes hold of my hand. 'I don't want her to die, Heather. What will we do? There are so many things I wanted to tell her.'

'You will always have me,' I say, squeezing her hand. 'And, hopefully, you still have time to tell her.'

CHAPTER 26

JESSIE

I still don't feel a hundred per cent safe and I doubt I'll sleep much tonight. The officer manning the police counter thought we were somewhat strange when we first described the posts on Facebook. Neither my mother nor I had screenshots. We finally had progress when he passed us to Detective Constable Shazia Nolan, who listened with interest. She'd previously dealt with a case where the father of three children told everyone he knew they had gone missing. He'd shared it on social media – their faces plastered online for the world to see. But they weren't missing. His wife and their three young daughters were in a shelter for victims of domestic abuse. Apparently, almost twenty per cent of the missing-people posts on social media aren't what they seem. Shazia said she'll contact Gloucestershire Constabulary with regard to the man seen outside my house and has asked them to carry out a welfare check on Mark. I pressed her on that because she warned us local police will probably think he's perfectly capable of looking after himself.

Me and Mum are on our sixth cup of tea, and we've been half-watching episodes of *Vera* that have merged into one, for me at least. We've talked for hours about who could possibly be doing this and we're still no closer to working it out. We'll just have to wait until the police get back to us. I keep checking my phone for news, but there's been nothing.

This is my second evening here but it feels like I've been here for weeks: it's claustrophobic. I feel hemmed in by the walls. A heavy cloud seems to cover me every time I walk inside, which is weird as I've never been here before yesterday. That I know of.

'Did I ever come to this house as a child?' I ask Mum.

Mum looks over the top of her Poundland reading glasses.

'Not that I know of,' she says, a slight smile on her face.

'Must be the bareness of it. Not that I'm judging your decoration,' I add quickly.

'I don't like having clutter,' she says. 'We are more than our possessions.'

She actually sounds serious.

'You what?'

'I'm kidding.' She scribbles on a corner of a magazine. 'Now shush. I think I know who the murderer is.'

My phone lights up with a message. It's been going off all afternoon, but I haven't read them because they're all from Mark's mum Judith. Shit. I haven't telephoned her back. With all that's going on, it really did slip my mind this time.

I glance as she sends through another paragraph. I hold the phone up to read the first few lines on my home screen.

'I didn't ring Mark's mother,' I tell Mum. 'She doesn't know I can't get hold of him. He mustn't be with them. She's talking about coming up here to see us. She thinks he's here.'

Mum sighs before pressing pause on the telly.

'You'd better ring her,' she says. 'Does she know what's going on with Mia?'

'Of course not. She practically hates me. She thinks I ruined her son's life. You know she always thought I was guilty, not that she'd ever say as much. She said she wants me to tell her what the hell's going on or she'll report Mark as missing. Which means the police haven't even been round to talk to her. They're not taking it seriously, are they?'

'Maybe he's followed you,' Mum suggests. 'Got a hire car so he won't be traced by these people he's involved with.'

'No. I'd have heard from him if he were. There'd be no reason to hide it from me.'

'Why would that be?' she asks. 'That you haven't heard from him, I mean.' She places the pen on the side table and rests her elbows on her knees. She leans forward. 'Now don't be cross at me, Jess. But I overheard you when you were in the bathroom.'

'Which bit did you hear?'

'You were talking to your friend Liza,' she says. 'You don't think he's having an affair with her, do you? She seems to be quite involved – going round to your house at all hours of the day and night.'

'You've let your imagination run away with you, Mum. They wouldn't do that to me. He thinks she's weird.'

I get up to peek through the curtains. There's nothing out of the ordinary outside. Next door's cat is sitting on Mum's front wall, keeping watch. You can't go wrong with cats. They don't need walking, constant attention, and they don't bark if the postman knocks. I feel a pang of disloyalty when I think of my gran's dog, Tilly. The only dog I ever loved. It was so old, and quiet and calm.

I let the curtain drop.

'There's no one out there,' I say. 'I'll call Mark's mum. Try to calm her down – see if she can go round there if the police haven't yet.'

'Good luck,' says Mum, raising her eyebrows over her glasses.

I head out to the back yard, the furthest away from Mia sleeping.

I'll give it three rings, and if she doesn't—

Shit.

'Hi, Judith,' I whisper. 'I know it's late...'

'I've been trying to call you all day,' she shrieks. Her household must be awake. If she's treating this like an emergency, she'll have both her neighbours round, too. 'Where are you? Have you heard from Mark?'

'I'm at my mum's.' I don't try to be quiet this time. 'Did Mark not tell you? I thought it'd be nice for Mia and me to get away.' I'm trying to minimise it – I don't know what he's told her.

'Of course he told me,' she says with a bristle. 'But it's not the school holidays yet, and I haven't heard from Mark since Sunday night. Has he contacted you?'

'No,' I say, relenting. There's no point hiding the fact that I'm worried about him, too. 'I've been trying to contact him for almost two days, but he hasn't replied.' Tears spring to my eyes – I collapse onto Mum's plastic chair. 'I told the police all of this this afternoon, but I haven't heard back from them – even though I've rung them twice since.'

'Oh God, Jessie,' she says, the panic evident in her voice. 'Shall we go round there to check on him?'

'I think that's a good idea,' I say. 'If you don't mind. I know it's so late.'

'It's my son,' she shrieks. 'I should've gone there earlier. My intuition is never wrong. Why didn't you tell me earlier, Jessie?'

'I...'

I can't tell her about the threats to Mia – it might send her over the edge. One problem at a time.

'Thanks for going round there, Judith,' I say. 'Will you let me know he's OK?'

'Of course.' She says it tersely. She's silent. 'Did you two argue before you went to your mum's?'

'What? No.'

'It does seem strange that you flee to your mother's and I haven't heard from my son since...'

'I haven't hurt him, Judith, if that's what you're getting at.'

'OK, OK,' she says. 'There's no need to shout at me. I'm worried – my thoughts have been everywhere.'

She'll never forget my past; she's always quick to believe the worst about me.

We say our goodbyes. If I were inside, I'd have thrown the phone onto the settee. I'm literally shaking. With fear, with anger.

I take two long deep breaths. *Calm, calm.*

'Hello?'

It's a voice from the garden next door. I stand on tiptoes to look over the short fence. It's that man – what's his name – having a cigarette, sitting on the back door step.

'I didn't know you were there,' I say, feeling the heat flood my face.

'I wasn't listening in.' He holds up his phone. 'I was playing *Toon Blast*.'

'Oh. OK.'

Of course he was listening in.

'I heard you pacing just then, though,' he says. 'That's the trouble with gravel. You can't walk anywhere quietly.'

'Just having a bit of family trouble. What are you doing outside at this time of the night?'

'Was having a few beers,' he says. 'Mum doesn't drink, so I save it for when she's gone to bed.'

'Oh, well, I'd better go back.'

I dash inside and shut the door, resting my back against it. He must think I'm awfully strange. Having harsh words on the phone at one thirty in the morning.

'What's happened?' Mum asks, shuffling down the hall in huge fluffy slippers.

'Judith,' I say, turning to lock the door. 'Hinting that she thinks I'm the reason that Mark's gone off-grid.'

'What?'

'Yeah.' I reach past Mum to get the milk. 'She thinks I've done something to him. How would I hurt a grown man?'

'So you didn't mention anything about Mia?'

'No, I didn't tell her.'

I rub my face; my body's exhausted but my mind is racing.

'I don't know why you're covering for him,' she says. 'What kind of person sees those sorts of posts on the internet about his own daughter, then does a bunk? A coward, that's what.'

'He won't have done that, Mum.'

She shrugs. Going by her experience with boyfriends, it's not surprising she doesn't believe me.

I glance at the clock.

'I'd better be getting to bed.'

'But we haven't seen who the murderer is!'

'You can tell me in the morning,' I say. 'To be honest, it's the last thing on my mind.'

'I didn't mean to minimise your problems, Jessie. I thought a good drama would take your mind off everything.'

I lean over to kiss her cheek.

'Night, night, Mum.'

CHAPTER 27

HEATHER

Mum is sleeping noisily on her side, and I'm lying on the reclining chair next to her. It reminds me of when Lauren was a baby. I'd lie and watch her sleeping, her cot just inches from my face. I was terrified that if I didn't keep my eye on her then she'd stop breathing. It was only pure exhaustion that allowed me a few hours' sleep at a time.

I don't know what I'm going to do without Mum. For years, I would pop round to hers every day. She was my rock when everything happened with Lauren. She came to court with me every day, holding my hand as they described the horrendous details of how my daughter died. The pictures of her body on the metal table in the morgue. The photographs of where I found her: the crime scene; the daisies and the buttercups were long gone.

I can't imagine life without my mother. Since she's been in this place, she's been half-gone for almost a year. In her mind, she seems somewhere else far away. It's like she's been withdrawing from us gradually to get us used to the idea of letting her go.

The doctor said the heart attack was mild, but after an ECG

they said it was the most recent of several. She must've had them in her sleep, he said. They might have happened months ago. I thought her apathy was psychological, but it was her body telling her to go easy. That it's slowly shutting down. It's so different to Dad. His heart got him in the middle of the day when he was at work. Imagine going out in the morning and never coming back. He was only forty-nine. I was twenty-one and Sadie was seventeen, and we were absolutely devastated. Heartbreak seems to follow me, but every day I thank God for Eddie and Sadie. I say, *God*. Maybe I'm thanking the universe. Maybe I'm thanking no one – just myself and my lucky stars. At least there's such things as stars.

'Heather.' Mum's whisper jolts my mind back into the room. 'Heather, it's you. I thought I heard you thinking.'

It must be the morphine making her woozy.

I reach my hand over to hers; it's cold. I can feel the bones so sharp under her thin, dry skin.

'Mum,' I say quietly. 'How are you feeling? Would you like a drink of water?'

'How long have you been here?' she asks.

'Since just before one this afternoon. You've been fast asleep. Sadie's over there, sleeping.'

Mum lifts her head up slightly to see my sister in the foetal position in the chair in the corner. I don't know how she's managed to fall asleep like that – the wooden arms must be digging into her side.

'Ah, that's nice,' says Mum. 'My two girls and me.'

'Do you want a drink of water?' I ask again.

I go to get up but she squeezes my hand tight.

'No, no,' she says. Her eyes are closed for longer than they're open. 'I just want to be here, like this, with you. My precious little girl.' Her words come out slowly. 'We decided on your name when we were in Scotland – your dad and me. We saw this most magnificent meadow that was covered in purple and white heather and we both knew right away that was what we were going to call you.'

'I love that story, Mum. How did you pick Sadie?'

'They spelt Sandie wrong at the registry office.' She opens her eyes and looks right at me. 'But don't tell her.'

'What?' I sit up. 'Are you kidding me?'

'I'm not.'

'But that wasn't the story. You always said it was after that Joan Crawford film.'

'Didn't want her thinking it was a mistake, did I?' Mum closes her eyes. 'She loves her name, doesn't she?'

'She does. She was the only one in the whole school called Sadie and she loved it. Said it was like being Madonna or Cher.'

'She's a one, isn't she?' says Mum. 'You will look after her, won't you? She always seems so unsettled. She never put proper roots down.'

'She likes it that way,' I say. 'You know how easily she gets bored. Her mind's always on the go. That's why she sleeps so well – she uses all her energy up.'

'She gets that from your dad. I think he used up too much of his energy. But unlike your dad, Sadie likes her sleep. He only slept four hours a night. I often wonder if he'd slept more, would he have lived longer? But that's by the by now.'

Mum closes her eyes.

After five minutes, she's fast asleep.

Sadie moves in the chair.

'Did Mum just wake up?' she asks, stretching.

'Just for a couple of minutes.'

'Why didn't you wake me?' she says. 'That might have been my only chance.'

'I'm sorry, Sadie, but she sounded fine. She might even be on the mend.'

She stands and walks towards the bed, bending down to take a good look at Mum's face.

'But they say that sometimes people are lucid for only a few minutes before they never regain consciousness.'

'Who says that?'

'Doctors.'

'Shall we wake her again?'

Sadie thinks for a moment, frowning.

'We can wait till the morning,' she says. 'The proper morning.'

She sits back on the chair and takes out her phone. It lights up her face.

I know what she's looking for: more information on Rosie McShane's daughter.

I don't want to hear it right now. I feel selfish thinking that. After reading Sadie's transcripts till the small hours, I'm ninety-nine per cent convinced of Rosie's innocence. Samantha Kasinski was adamant she was with Rosie just minutes before I found Lauren – even decades later. Sadie told me Samantha was prepared to put it down in a statement, should a new investigation be opened.

This, added with the not-so-subtle hints that Mark Donovan was a wrong 'un – plying young girls with alcohol in order to... To do what? There's no evidence to suggest it was more than kids messing about. And why would he threaten to abduct and harm his very own child? It doesn't make sense and I shouldn't be thinking about this when I should be thinking of my mum, who might not have long left on this earth.

'All the posts about Mia have been deleted,' says Sadie. 'I can't find any of them.' She's scrolling, scrolling. 'A newspaper has picked it up, though – some guy called Jonathan Ainsworth. The speed online journos can churn out articles is unbelievable. He's quoted my hypothesis of there being a serial killer, which he's linked to Mia Donovan's so-called disappearance. At least someone is taking my theories seriously. That bloke might be a proper journalist after all.'

'Do you want a hot drink?' I stand, and go over to my bag to get some change.

'Hot chocolate, please,' she says without looking up.

I open the door to the twilight of the corridor. Most of the doors are closed, except for a room I pass where a man is being read to. I want to stand and listen to the story, too. The woman reading looks up at me. There's only one reason we're here at this time of night, and we share a small smile before I head towards the vending machine.

When I get back, Sadie still has her face in her phone. I place the drinks on the small table and pick up the little notebook on Mum's bedside cabinet. Inside are Mum's handwritten notes. I shouldn't read it, but I feel compelled when I see my dad's name written at the top of one of the pages.

David sat at the end of my bed. He said he's waiting for me.

There are ten or so similar sentences saying my father is telling her it's going to be all right. I turn the page to see Lauren's name.

Lauren says she sends butterflies to her mummy.

She says that the rainbow I saw yesterday was her saying hello.

My heart gives a jolt when I see the last entry.

Lauren says they need to keep searching and that they're close.

I slam the book shut. The date of these entries was just over two weeks ago. Mum was suffering with a horrible UTI. They can lead to hallucinations if left untreated for a length of time. This would explain the things and people she thought she could see. Mum never complains, even when she's in terrible pain.

I sit beside her and stroke her cheek.

If the words she thinks Dad and Lauren said give her some comfort then I'm not going to tell her otherwise. Who gets to decide what's real in someone else's mind?

My phone vibrates with a message; I retrieve it from my bag.

'Message from Eddie,' I tell Sadie. He's been texting every hour or so – he knows I'd not be able to sleep much in here. 'Oh.'

Sadie sits up, her interest piqued.

'He said that someone's outside Marie McShane's new house. It's a man in his forties. Tall, longish hair.' I look up. 'How does Eddie know where she lives now?'

'I've no idea,' she says. 'Maybe he followed them yesterday when he saw them in the park.'

'He wouldn't do something like that. Just because *you'd* think nothing of following someone, doesn't mean *he* would.'

'He's going through a lot, Heather,' she says. 'Didn't you see how stressed he was last night? What we're going through with Mum right now is sending him back to being with his own mother last year. Couple that with the fact he's only just learned that Lauren's killer is still out there... Well, it's bound to cause anyone in their right mind to act out of character.'

'Oh.'

Sadie has always been spot-on at reading people. I suppose being perceptive – interpreting what's lying underneath the surface of a person and what they're saying – is part of her job.

'This man outside Marie's house,' I say. 'Is it Mark? Will Eddie be in any danger if he approaches him? I knew he wouldn't listen when we told him not to try to find him.' Another message comes through. 'He's sent a picture.'

'Can you forward it to me?' Sadie asks.

I glance at Mum – still sound asleep – before sending her the photo.

'I have no idea who that is,' she says. 'The picture's too grainy and it's too dark outside to make out any features. Eddie won't get into trouble if he just stays in his car like I... Why is the man peeking through the window like that? Do you think it's one of Marie's boyfriends?' She looks up at me. 'Sorry, I'm just thinking out loud.'

'You're not asking the most obvious question,' I say. 'Which is: what the hell is Eddie doing sitting outside Marie McShane's house?'

CHAPTER 28
JESSIE

Wednesday, 13th March

The sound of Mia's scream is what wakes me. I'm lying on the floor under a couple of settee cushions and they part as I dive towards the single bed my daughter has taken over.

She's still sleeping but a tear is running down the side of her face and onto the pillow. Is it Mark she's dreaming of? Have I underestimated how much she's been listening to me talking about him and our situation?

I wipe the tear from her little face. I can only shield her for so long. She's still so young. She might forget that we had it almost perfect for a while.

I was the same age as Mia when my father left us. Well, that's what my mum says. I can't even remember his face. There are no photographs, no members of his family around to remind me. I think his name was Charlie, but I can't remember that, either. I know I should be more curious about him, but it's hard to care about someone who's never given me a second thought.

Mia sniffles in her sleep.

My darling little girl. She was the one who changed my life;

gave me purpose. When she was born, it was the first time I'd ever cried with happiness. Seeing her scrunched-up little face as she came out screaming. The way she looked at me when she first opened her eyes – like we'd known each other for a thousand lifetimes.

She's shaking her head, thrashing it against the pillow.

'No,' she says. 'Don't do that.' Another tear runs down her face. 'Please don't do that, Marie.'

I gently squeeze her shoulder.

'Mia,' I say softly. 'Mia, wake up. It's just a dream.'

Her lashes flutter before she opens her eyes. She wipes them with her fist and sits up quickly.

'Oh, Mummy,' she says, wrapping her arms around my neck.

'Are you all right?' I stroke her hair, damp from sweat at the neck. 'Did you have a nightmare?'

'Yes,' she whispers in my ear. 'Marie tied me up and then she was going to put a pillow over my face, and that's when you saved me, Mummy.'

Her whole body shakes as she cries into the crook of my neck.

'It's OK, love,' I say. 'It's not real. Granny will never hurt you.'

'She's not my granny,' she says. 'She's Marie. My real granny is at home with Daddy. Please can we go home? I miss my house. I miss Daddy.'

'Soon,' I say. 'Soon we can.'

'I don't want to stay in the house again today,' she says, pulling away from me and sitting up.

'But we went to the park yesterday.'

'But that was only for twenty minutes before Marie started arguing with that nice lady.'

'How do you know she was nice?'

'Because she talked to me before she came and sat next to

you.'

'What?'

'She asked me where I came from. But I didn't tell her, Mummy, because she was still a stranger then. So I told her we were from London and we were visiting my gran. Was that OK?'

'Of course that's OK. But next time, sweetie, if someone tries to talk to you and you don't know them, come straight to me.'

'OK, Mummy,' she says earnestly. 'I will do that.' She pauses, her right eyebrow raises. 'Mummy?'

'What?'

'Can we go to get a milkshake today? What day is it? Am I meant to be in school?'

'It's Wednesday. It's almost the school holidays. I'll ask Marie if there's anywhere we can go for a milkshake.'

'Can we go on our own, please, Mummy. Just me and you?'

She makes a fist and gently rolls it in the crook of my arm – something she used to do for comfort that she hasn't done in months.

'Of course.' I put the bed cover over her lap. 'Do you want a little lie-in today?'

She whips it off.

'No. I don't like dreaming any more. I'm not tired. Can we go to the milkshake café now?'

I smile. 'It's only half past six, love,' I say, standing. 'Come on, let's go and watch some cartoons.'

She holds my hand as she slides off the bed.

'I'm too old for cartoons,' she says. 'I'm almost five.'

'OK.' Even though I'm sure she was watching *Paw Patrol* yesterday. 'What about *Horrible Histories*?'

'Ugh, no. That's gross. That's for eight-year-olds. I might be sick with it.'

Unsurprisingly the rest of the house is silent. Mum never was an early riser.

In the living room, daylight is streaming through the light-weight orange curtains. As we move to the settee, specks of dust flow through the air.

'Little fairies,' says Mia, lightly, suggesting she's forgotten her nightmare.

She picks up the remote for the TV and expertly navigates to *CBeebies*. When I was her age, I never had control of the television. If it wasn't my brother, it was one of the blokes Mum had round at the time. One of them used to stay up all night watching television in his underpants. Disgusting man. Around children as well.

There's a bang that seems to come from the back garden.

'I'll just get you some juice,' I say to an engrossed Mia.

I don't know why I'm tiptoeing. If someone's trespassing I want them gone by the time I reach the back door.

My heart is thumping.

I'm praying it's just a cat or a bird.

I can't see anything from the kitchen window.

It'll be nothing.

I take hold of the door handle, take a deep breath, and pull it open.

'Mum!'

She's at the end of the garden, a trowel in her hand, peering over the back gate.

'I saw him again,' she says, not turning around. 'I thought we'd be safe here, but we're not. I tell you, Jessie, it's him. That Eddie guy. He won't stop until...'

'What?' I move closer, so as not to shout and wake the neighbours. 'He won't stop until what?'

'He's gone. Did you hear that?'

'No. Hear what?' I take hold of her hand. 'Mum, do you

know what time it is? No one's going to be sneaking around here. Why would they want to find us?'

She turns and rests her hands on my shoulders.

'I think we should leave,' she says. 'We should go back to your house. We'll be safe there. They won't know where to find...' Two birds flap their wings at each other on next door's roof. 'We should leave this morning. Mia will be pleased. I don't think she likes being here.'

'OK,' I say. 'I need to find out what's going on with Mark.'

'Yes. We can stay at yours for a few days, maybe even a few weeks. It'll be like a holiday. You've such a lovely house. Even though I've never been invited to stay before.'

'Let's go inside,' I say, trying to pull her gently from the gate. 'We'll wake the neighbours at this rate.'

'Mummy!' Mia's standing at the back door. 'Mummy, come here.'

'Coming,' I say. 'Come on, Mum. You're scaring Mia.'

'There's someone at the door,' says Mia in a dramatic whisper, walking towards the front door. 'He looked through the letterbox. He knows my name. He said "Hello, Mia. Can you let me in?" but I didn't because of what you said about strangers before.' Her eyes widen and she holds out her hands. 'Who is it?'

Mum and I jump when there's a knock at the door.

'I *told* you,' says Mia, taking hold of my hand.

'Who could be knocking at this time?' I ask Mum. 'It's not even seven.'

'There's only one way to find out,' she says, pushing Mia and me aside.

She opens the door.

There, standing with his arms open, wearing jogging bottoms with a silk bomber jacket, is my brother Billy.

CHAPTER 29

JESSIE

'Why didn't you tell me you were coming?' says Mum, rushing to give Billy a hug. 'Oh my word, I can't believe it. Come in, come in.'

He grabs a giant backpack that's half the size of him and lugs it inside.

He rubs the top of my head before grabbing me in a hug.

'Jessie Jess,' he says, pulling away, still holding me by the tops of my arms. He kisses my cheek. There's a hint that he's been crying: his eyes are watery and red. He's never greeted me this emotionally before. 'I've missed you so much, Jessie.' He bends down to a bewildered Mia at my side. 'And this must be my favourite niece in the whole world. Are you going to give Uncle Billy a hug?'

She shakes her head slowly.

'No worries,' he says, laughing. 'There's plenty of time for that.'

'Are you staying long, then?' Mum asks Billy. 'Does this mean you're visiting for more than a week this time?'

'It might,' he says. 'Shall I put the kettle on? Came straight from the airport. Flew down from Aberdeen – flight was meant to be at midnight but was delayed three hours as usual. I'm absolutely shattered.'

'I can't believe you didn't give me a clue you were coming,' says Mum, linking Billy's arm and leading him into the kitchen.

I take Mia by the hand and guide her into the living room.

'Who's that?' she asks, climbing onto the settee.

'It's my brother Billy.'

'The one from Scotland?'

Her eyes are wide again – even though she's been to Scotland a handful of times, she's still impressed that he's come from another country. She must be completely overwhelmed with what's happened in such a short space of time.

'That's right,' I say. 'He's been travelling for a few hours. I don't think he knew we were here.'

'I bet they get snow at Christmas in Scotland,' she says earnestly. 'Can we go to Uncle Billy's one Christmas so I can build a snowman?'

'I'm sure we will one day.'

Mum brings through a tray of tea and biscuits; I think she still likes the ceremony of tea in a teapot.

'You still off the sauce, Mum?' says Billy, plonking himself down in her chair. 'What's it been? Six months? The longest six months of your life, no doubt.'

'Yes,' she says. 'Very funny.'

He gets away with more cheek than I ever could. It's always been like that.

'Proud of you, Mum,' he says, grabbing a mug and taking a gulp.

I take mine and blow on it.

'Your mouth's made of asbestos,' I say.

'You know it!' he says, smiling. 'Tea has to be hot. Otherwise what's the point of it? It's disgusting cold.'

'Did you leave your fiancée back at home?' Mum asks.

I watch my brother's reaction, but he simply shrugs.

'Changed my mind about the whole thing,' he says. 'Being tied to a woman, let alone another country, wasn't for me.'

'What about the baby?' I say.

'Eh? Oh, that. It was a false alarm. I'm too young for all that fatherhood business, anyway.'

'You're forty-five.'

'Thanks for the reminder, sis,' he says, rolling his eyes. 'Youth is an attitude, not just a number.'

He grabs a digestive biscuit and dunks it in his tea.

I haven't seen him for so long, he's almost a stranger. He seems taller and thinner than when I last saw him two years ago.

'How long were you two together?' I ask.

'About eighteen months,' he says. 'She works in HR. Pretty boring, to be honest. She's a very serious person. Too serious for me. Talked about pensions and shit like that.' He glances at Mia. 'Sorry, kid.' He looks at me. 'Sorry, Jess. Not used to being round little ears.'

'Mummy, can I play on your phone?' Mia slides off the settee. 'Can I take it in the other room?'

'Of course.' I place the mug down and walk her to the bedroom. She settles herself onto the bed. 'It's still only early. You relax there. Let me know if any messages come through for me, won't you?'

'I will.'

Back in the living room, Mum and Billy have their heads close together. They stop talking as I sit.

'Were you talking about me?'

It used to happen all the time. Especially the days in between the police interviews. Twelve years old, being grilled by the police, then coming home to find my own family talking and whispering about me in corners. Looking at me as though I were a stranger they didn't know how to speak to.

'I was telling Billy about the missing posts on Facebook,'

Mum explains. 'In fact, I told him about it when I first saw it on Monday. I wondered why you hadn't replied, Billy. Couldn't you get a signal at the airport?'

'Is that why you came home?' I ask.

'I didn't want to say it in front of Mia,' he says. 'But I've been worried sick, not being able to get a signal in the air. Thank God she's here, safe.'

'She might not be safe,' says Mum, picking up her mobile phone. 'I found another one.'

'What?' Billy takes the phone. 'That can't be right.' He looks up. 'The police know about this, right?'

I nod.

'And where's Mark in all of this?' he asks. 'Do you think he's behind it? Mum said you had some sort of falling out.'

'No. We haven't fallen out. I'm fed up of having to say it. He knows where Mia is. He doesn't need to try to find her. He stopped at home to sort out some business.'

'Where the hell is he, then? He should be here protecting his family.'

'I don't know where he is,' I say quietly. 'Can you keep your voice down, please? I don't want Mia getting worried.'

'Sorry.' Billy takes off his boots. 'It's just typical of him to go running when there's a crisis. Bloody typical.'

'What happened between you two?' I say.

Mum stands.

'I'll get you another tea, Billy,' she says. She lingers at the door. 'I can't believe I have my two children with me under the same roof after all these years.'

'Has Mum been OK?' Billy asks when she's out of earshot. 'I can't believe she's stopped drinking. Do you think she's really given it up?'

'From what I've seen in the past couple of days, I'd say yes.'

'Well, bloody hell,' he says. 'After all these years. Who'd have thought it?'

'I know. At least Mia can have a sober grandmother. Not like us who had a—'

'A wasted mother.'

'Billy! I can't believe you just said that.'

'Why?' He glances around the room. 'Our childhood was horrendous.' He says it so matter-of-fact. 'She spent all her money on booze, and we had to bloody steal to get food.'

'We did?'

'Well, I did.'

'Sorry, Billy,' I say, staring at the carpet. 'I always thought you'd just found money.'

He rubs the top of my head again.

'I didn't want you to think I was a thief, did I?'

He stares at the closed curtains and tuts. He stands and whips them open.

'They were always shut, weren't they?' he says, sitting back down. 'We were always in the shade. God, do you remember that arsehole Davy who used to live with us?'

'Arsehole?' I say. 'I thought he was nice. He was always kind to me.'

'He wasn't bloody nice to me. Used to slap me around, the prick. Didn't like another male in the house standing up to him. I remember that godawful holiday in Scarborough. He beat the actual shit out of me in front of Mark. It was bloody mortifying. Imagine that? A fifteen-year-old boy getting slapped around in front of his best mate. I'm lucky Mark didn't spread it around. And Davy was built like a fucking brick shithouse. I was never going to win that fight. No. That bloke was a piece of shit. Plying our mother with drink so he could get her wages. Useless wanker. If I saw him now, I'd—'

'We've still got some of these party rings left,' says Mum, totally oblivious. 'Did you use to like them, too, Billy?'

'I guess.'

His rant about Davy seems to have tired him out. I

genuinely cannot remember him being so horrible to Billy. My poor brother having to deal with that, but also protecting me from the reality – making sure I always had something to eat. It makes me sad that we've not really had a relationship since. Our lives might've been different had we been closer. I lost a lot of people – friends, family, on that awful day in 1994.

There's a knock at the door.

Mum stands, just after she sits.

'It's like Piccadilly Circus in here this morning,' she says almost jogging out the room. When she opens the front door, there's a moment of silence before she says, 'Oh. It's you.'

'I'd like to speak to Jessie,' says a woman's voice.

'Wait there,' says Mum.

Mum passes me as I head to the hallway.

'Who is it?' I whisper, but Mum's already in the living room.

I pull the front door fully open.

It's a face I haven't seen for years. The only person who thought I was innocent. The person who's been on my mind for these past couple of days. Finally, someone able to help me. The person with a nose and the curiosity to find the truth.

'Sadie Harrison,' I say. 'I've never been so happy to see you.'

CHAPTER 30

HEATHER

I can't believe Sadie asked Eddie to keep a watch over Marie McShane's house. It's one thing to doubt Rosie as my daughter's murderer, but to actively task my husband to keep watch over her mother is a step too far.

I've pretended to be asleep ever since she told me. I admit I've calmed down a little, now, and my heart doesn't race as much whenever I catch myself thinking about it. Plus, it wouldn't be right to have a full-blown argument in front of Mum – even though she's not woken since three this morning.

It's almost seven – the doctor's due in an hour. Hopefully we can get some definite answers. Mum's eighty-two, but she doesn't seem old enough to be slipping away from us. I look up to the ceiling. *Please let her be OK. Please let her have a few more years with us.* Maybe she could move in with Eddie and me. We could sell up and get a nice bungalow to make life easier for her.

'Heather.' Sadie's nudging my arm. 'Heather, wake up.'

'What is it?' I say grumpily, sitting up. 'What time is it?'

'It's seven,' she says. 'Mum woke after you fell asleep. About two hours ago.'

'What? I wouldn't have slept through that.'

'You were exhausted. Just because you're the eldest, it doesn't mean you have to control everything. I'm allowed to talk to Mum without you listening in.'

'I don't want to control everything,' I say, not hiding the sting I feel in my voice. 'I'm surprised I slept through it, that's all.'

She glances at Mum before gesturing me to follow her out the room.

I stand, letting the blanket slip to the floor.

'What is it?'

There are two patients walking slowly along the corridor.

'Don't be so cross with me,' says Sadie. 'I've done nothing wrong.'

'This is a time for Mum,' I say sharply. 'Not a time to be distracted by Rosie McShane. All I'm asking is that we don't talk about it around Mum.'

'I'm not like you,' she says gently. 'I have to be distracted. I can't put all my focus onto Mum dying, because it's breaking my heart.'

Tears start to fall down her face.

'God, I'm sorry, Sadie.' I rub the top of her arm. 'I know you're not like me. I'm glad you're not like me.'

She wipes her face with the sleeve of her jumper.

'Did you know Mum was keeping a diary?' she says.

'You mean that notebook on her bedside table?'

Sadie nods.

'Yes,' I say. 'Like a dream diary.'

'When I spoke to her in the night she said it's messages from Dad and Lauren.'

'Don't tell me you believe that?' My head jolts back. 'You're always going on about provable facts.'

'No, I'm not saying I believe that,' she says. 'Mum does, though. She made me promise her something.'

'What's that? I hope you're not going to use this as an excuse to leave.'

'Heather!'

'That's what it is, isn't it? You're taking advantage of Mum's fragile state of mind to go chasing after...' I lower my voice. 'Let's be honest, here. Rosie is a convicted killer.'

'Mum thinks Rosie's innocent.'

'Now you're just making things up, Sadie.'

'No, really. She said she never believed that a little girl could kill another.'

'Well, twelve members of the public were certainly convinced.'

'Rosie should never have been tried as an adult.'

'Stop right there, Sadie.' My heart is beating so fast I think I might collapse. 'You're going too far, now.'

She strides into Mum's room and comes out with her bag.

'I'll just be an hour, tops,' she says. 'Mum will be fine with you.'

'But Sadie...' I'm talking to her back now. 'What if she...?'

She turns around.

'I'll make it,' she says. 'I promise. An hour.' She clasps her hands in a pleading gesture before running out the door.

I walk back into Mum's room, adrenaline causing my hands to shake.

To look at her now, you'd think she was fine. Just sleeping; she'll wake at any time.

I sit at the end of her bed as her eyes flutter under her lids.

'What are you dreaming about, Mum?' I say. 'If you're dreaming about Lauren, tell her I love her.'

CHAPTER 31

SADIE

15th August 2020

Sadie Harrison – Investigative Journalist

Interview with Samantha Kasinski (Sam)

Location: via Zoom.

Time: 23:10

SH: If the connection goes again, I'll telephone you instead.

Sam: Sure, that's fine.

SH: How's the weather over there in Montreal?

Sam: Probably the same as it is over there. Bit sunny, bit cloudy.

SH: (laughs) That sounds about right, though it's night-time here now. Shall we just get into it? Are you still fine with being recorded?

Sam: Just as long as you don't show the video to anyone (laughs). I'm just kidding. I brushed my hair especially.

SH: When we talked earlier, I asked you to recall what happened in March 1994. Are you OK going through it all again?

Sam: Yes. It's a long time ago – what – almost thirty years? Jeez, I can't believe that.

SH: I know.

Sam: I used to visit my grandmother's house every so often – holidays, some weekends. We lived about half an hour away in Cheshire. I have good memories of visiting there, of playing with Rosie. I wasn't as close to Lauren, though. She didn't seem to like me much. I was into messing about, climbing trees, that sort of thing. Lauren loved talking about boys. That's what I remember most about her. She had a crush on one of the boys. Mark, his name was – is. I have no idea what he's doing now.

SH: He's married now, I think.

Sam: Well, that's not surprising. We're in our forties now. Though, he probably married someone twenty years younger (laughs).

SH: What makes you say that?

Sam: Because he was into the younger ones. I know we were only a few years younger than him, but it was the way he liked to... I don't know. Girls their own age never seemed to pay them any attention. It was really weird, that time.

SH: In what way?

Sam: Did my grandmother tell you what happened with them? The boys?

SH: She told me what happened with Mark – that he tried to get you drunk.

Sam: We were playing hide and seek – I was probably the one who instigated the game. Lauren had gone into the field… she sat right in the middle of it… said the whole game was babyish. She probably wasn't getting enough attention. Anyway, I was halfway up a tree when the boys came up to me, saying they'd found me. They weren't even in on the game. They said if I went with them, they'd show me an even better hiding place. I recognised Rosie's brother, Billy, so I thought I'd be OK.

SH: Billy?

Sam: Yes, that's right.

SH: Are you sure it was him?

Sam: Yeah. I'd seen him before. Had a bit of a crush on him actually. Which was why, when they said I could have some of their drink, I drank some.

SH: Did you know there was alcohol in it?

Sam: Kinda. They were older, you know? They wouldn't just be drinking orange juice, would they?

SH: I suppose.

Sam: They had a two-litre bottle of it. I think it was vodka they mixed in with it. I guess I was trying to impress Billy when I took more than a few gulps of it.

SH: Where were Lauren and Rosie?

Sam: I didn't know where Rosie was at the time, but Lauren was still in the field.

SH: What time was this, can you remember?

Sam: No, I don't remember any of the times. The afternoon blurred into the evening.

SH: Was Lauren still sitting up, or was she lying down when you saw her in the field?

Sam: She was doing cartwheels and handstands. I recall that because I remember thinking that she called me babyish for playing hide and seek when she herself was doing cartwheels. God, I'm so sorry about what happened to her. I wish she'd have come with me, then it'd never have happened.

SH: What makes you so sure about that?

Sam: Well, I got pretty drunk, and Mark kept trying to kiss me. It was a bit creepy, to be honest. He had this look in his eyes.

SH: What kind of look?

Sam: Like he'd been taken over, possessed. Sorry that's just my child brain saying that. But it's what I've always thought.

SH: What happened after you felt a bit tipsy, after Mark tried to kiss you?

Sam: Billy sort of tagged behind as Mark guided me to this weird stick hut type thing. It was like a teepee made of branches and leaves and stuff. He grabbed me by the waist, tried to get me inside. That's when she saved me.

SH: Who saved you?

Sam: Rosie. She was sitting inside the hut, waiting to be found. Mark swore at her – asking what the hell she was doing in his den. She was almost crying – and I was hysterical. I thought I was being kidnapped.

SH: That sounds terrifying, Sam.

Sam: Everything's magnified when you're a kid – the forest seemed denser, the boys seemed like men. Even though I was tipsy – actually I was pretty drunk because that was the first time I'd tried alcohol – I remember everything as though it were yesterday. If Rosie wasn't there – and I often wonder this – if she wasn't… Then it might have been me and not Lauren who died that day.

SH: What are you saying? I don't understand.

Sam: She helped me back to my house – to my grandmother's house. She was so worried about me.

SH: But Rosie was found guilty of killing Lauren. Do you think it was one of the boys?

Sam: I don't know, but if you compare the likelihood of it being them with it being a twelve-year-old girl, I'd say the odds were pretty high.

SH: Your grandmother said you told the police that Rosie was with you when Lauren was harmed.

Sam: Yes, I told the police when they came round. I told them about Mark, and then I told them about Rosie walking me home. I was in trouble a bit as a kid – my brothers were always leading me astray and they were quicker to run away when a grown-up came along. The woman at the corner shop made an example of me when she found three Mars bars missing. She kept me in the back room and called the police. I was petrified. The policeman gave me a stern telling off. It was the same officer who came to the house after my grandmother called them. They thought I was making up stories – that I'd stolen sherry from my grandmother's cabinet and was trying to pin the blame on someone else. He didn't take me seriously because there had already been a call about Lauren. And when I told him Rosie had been with me, he thought I was lying to protect her. I said that Rosie can't have hurt her because she screamed about a minute after she left my house, but he was having none of it.

SH: Why do you think the police were quick to believe it was Rosie?

Sam: There was no one else around when Lauren's mum found them. Poor Rosie. She was so kind. Such a gentle soul. She'd do anything for anyone. And her family – well… She was kind *despite* them. Horrible people.

SH: Why do you say that?

Sam: Her mother was either out, or in her own world. She used to sit on the doorstep on one of those camping chairs, drinking beer and smoking cigarettes. I'd have been mortified if that were my mum.

SH: She worked two jobs. She was a single parent raising two children.

Sam: I'm only going on what I saw.

SH: Who do you think killed Lauren Jones?

Sam: Either Mark or Billy. (...) My parents were absolutely devastated by what happened. They always said that it could've been me. They didn't let me out the house alone for months after it happened. It's why they wanted to move to Canada – less people, less chance of anything happening to me.

SH: Mark and Billy had alibis.

Sam: What do you mean?

SH: They were both at home when it happened.

Sam: How can that be? I saw them.

SH: It's what their parents said. Both their mothers vouched for them being at home.

Sam: They did? (...) Right, well. I guess one – or both – of their mothers was lying. I'm convinced it wasn't Rosie who killed Lauren. Convinced.

CHAPTER 32

JESSIE

'It's good to see you, Jessie,' says Sadie.

'It's good to see you, too,' I say. 'Are you in the area visiting Heather?'

'Yes, sort of. I've seen the news reports about your daughter.'

Sadie looks so much older than I remember, but then, I haven't seen her in a long time. The last time we talked it was over the phone. Her short hair is in the same style – the one she said was easy to look after – and is now a vibrant shade of red. She's not wearing a scrap of make-up, but she only has a few wrinkles. She must spend most of the time inside.

'News reports?' I say. 'I thought it was only on social media.'

'One of the local newspapers picked it up,' she says. 'Is Mia there? Is she OK?'

I step outside, wrapping my cardigan tightly around me, the wind whipping my hair across my face.

'She's fine. My brother's only just got here.' I look behind to check Mia hasn't come to find me. 'I was just thinking about you. I was hoping you'd be able to help me find out who's behind it all. My husband Mark received a message the other day suggesting whoever it is knows my birth name. They threatened to expose me.'

'Legally they can't,' she says. 'If they're based in the UK, at least.'

I'm not sure if it's the wind, but her eyes are red, brimming with tears.

'Are you OK?' I say. 'I don't mean to be rude, but you look terrible.'

She wipes her face with her sleeve.

'My mother's not well,' she says. 'We don't think she has long left.'

'Oh, Sadie. I'm so sorry to hear that.'

'It's not just that,' she adds. 'I spoke to a woman the other day...' She glances through the living-room window. Billy and Mum turn away; they were obviously looking, trying to hear what Sadie's got to say. 'Is it OK if we go for a walk?'

I close the front door.

'You know I interviewed your mum?' she says quietly.

'You did?' I say. 'When?'

'Almost twenty years ago. I thought you knew – you told me that she'd want paying, and she did.'

'She didn't mention it to me. I bet she can't remember what she said.' I turn around and move close to the window to catch Mum's eye. I signal that I'm going for a walk, and Mum puts her thumbs up. 'I can't be long,' I say to Sadie. 'Mia's inside, playing with my phone.'

'That's fine.'

* * *

We walk down the path and out the gate, turning right.

'I haven't been down this street for years,' says Sadie. 'Do you remember the youth club that used to be on the corner?'

'Not really.'

'I dropped Lauren off there once when you were in junior school. It's been demolished since. Unsafe temporary building. There used to be a lot of them.'

'I'm sure you didn't drag me out the house to talk about derelict buildings, Sadie.'

'No.'

She sounds so nervous. She's always been so confident, sure of herself.

'Have you ever spoken to Samantha?' she asks. 'The girl you used to play with when—'

'I know who Samantha is. I haven't seen her for years. Have you seen her?'

'A couple of years ago. I finally tracked her down. Took me a while, but I've had to take on various full-time desk jobs over the years to pay the bills.'

'Did you ever marry?' I ask. 'You never spoke about yourself much, from what I remember.'

'I had a few relationships, but none of them took.' She smiles. 'I have a lovely little cottage just outside York.' Her hair blows across her cheeks as her gaze stops at a boarded-up shop on the corner. 'I never could settle around here.'

'I'm not surprised,' I say. 'How is Samantha doing?'

'Really well.'

'No one took a minute's notice of me when I said I was with her.'

'I know they didn't,' she says. 'She says that Mark and Billy got her drunk.'

'What?' I stop walking. 'She didn't say it was them who'd given her the drink. Though, thinking back, we barely had a chance to speak. She was really freaked out. Why would they do that to a kid? They were three years older than us.'

'I've no idea why,' says Sadie. 'But they have form, don't they? Remember what you wrote in your diary about Lila?'

'What? No. I don't.' I take a step away from her. 'What diary?'

'The one you kept just before you started high school.' She reaches into her bag and takes out a small notebook. It's covered in childish shapes, drawn in pen. 'This is it.'

She holds it out, and I take it from her.

'There's a bench around the corner,' I say. 'I need to sit down for this.'

Once we're sitting, I open the cover and I feel a rush of warm familiarity as I read my ten-year-old self's handwriting. Boys, friends, school. Just a short time before everything went wrong, before everything turned bad. Back when I didn't know my life as I knew it was so precarious.

'Where did you get this?' I ask, blinking, but the tears fall after a gust of wind hits my face.

'Your mum gave it to me,' she says.

'What? My mother?' I feel winded, but I shouldn't be so surprised. 'I suppose you paid her for it?'

'Yes. It was when I interviewed her. To be fair to her, she didn't know the diary was in there. She thought she was lending me the books you read as a child. Inside it you described your connection to Lila. How Mark got her drunk and then dumped her on the doorstep of her parents' caravan.'

'Lila,' I say, my mind conjuring the image of her long sandy-coloured hair; us sitting in a field together making daisy chains; swinging our legs at the end of the pier, eating bags of chips that went cold too quickly in the freezing rain. 'I haven't thought about her in years. Have you spoken to her, too?'

'I'm sorry, Jessie,' she says. 'I thought you knew.'

A car passes us but avoids the giant puddle near the kerb.

'What happened to her?' I say, only half-wanting to know.

'She went missing in 1993 – not long after you met her in Scarborough.'

'Why didn't anyone tell me?'

'Your brother and Mark were questioned by police from what I gathered from your mum, but she didn't go into great detail. I don't know why they didn't tell you. Her body wasn't discovered until almost a year later when you were already in—'

'Where was she found?'

I cling to my diary as though somehow I'm holding the memory of Lila.

'In an abandoned house in Scarborough. She was only found because it was sold and was in the process of being demolished. Police haven't found her killer. Also... in 2003, there was a girl called Katie Masters who—'

'I remember us talking about it,' I interrupt. 'She lived in the same town as I did when I was released from Castleton.'

'And police spoke to you at the time when they were doing door to door.'

'I was under the care of my probation officer back then.'

'Can you remember if Mark or your brother visited you around that time?'

'They used to visit all the time,' I say. 'Separately, though. Why?'

'I think there's a strong case that either your husband Mark or your brother Billy has been the one committing these crimes against young girls. Another girl was found dead; her body posed – flowers in her hair. She was called Paige Lewis. She was twelve years old. This was in 2001 – when you were at Castleton.'

'No. I've never heard of a Paige Lewis.' I stand, still cradling my diary. 'It can't be Mark. He's my husband; my child's father. And it can't be Billy. My mum said he was at home – that he'd rushed there after Samantha cried all the way to her grandmother's house. Billy said he was afraid of getting into trouble with her parents. And Mark – his mum said he was home, too.'

'Did you never wonder how they got home so quickly?'

'No,' I say. 'I believed them. Neither of them would have let me get into so much trouble.'

'Let me guess,' she says dryly. 'Mark's been the perfect gentleman since – your protector. Wouldn't let anything – well, anything *else* at least – happen to you.'

'You've twisted everything.'

'And after you dropped Samantha off that awful day, you went into the field and saw Lauren lying in the middle of the field with her arms wide open? Flowers in her hair? You said Lila was fond of making daisy chains. Did she rebuff Mark in some way?' She visibly shivers. 'God, saying that about a child feels horrendous...'

'But it couldn't have been Mark or Billy.'

'I don't know for sure which one it is,' says Sadie. 'But someone's obviously lying.'

I turn to face the wind, wishing it would take me with it, away from this conversation I wish I'd never agreed to.

'You're one of the few people who didn't think it was me who killed Lauren,' I say. 'Did you ever doubt my innocence?'

'Perhaps at the beginning. Before I saw you in court,' she says, barely meeting my eye. 'You looked so small standing there. Bewildered. You didn't know what was going on and you'd just lost your best friend – the only one who would've been truly there for you. I've listened to your tapes twice over these past couple of days. I've re-read my transcripts of everyone I interviewed. The only people who wouldn't talk to me were Mark Donovan and Billy McShane.'

'I can't be married to Lauren's killer,' I say into the wind. 'I can't be the sister of a serial killer. There has to be someone else. Someone you missed.' The wind batters more tears from my eyes. 'But you've been working on this case for thirty years, haven't you?'

She turns her body towards me, holds one of my hands in hers.

'I'm so sorry, Jessie.'

* * *

It would be a lie to say that I could believe Sadie so easily, but she's been searching for so long for what really happened that day. She deserves a lot of credit for that. But what she's saying about Mark and Billy can't be true. That one of them – or both of them – has lied to my face, stood aside while I went through the hell of not only losing my best friend, but being convicted of, and punished for, her murder.

'I'd offer you to come inside,' I say as we reach my mother's house, 'but—'

'I'd love to,' says Sadie, walking to the front door. 'Thanks, Jessie.'

'Oh,' I say. 'OK.'

She's braver than I am. Sadie has never hidden what she thinks about my mother. She's lucky Mum isn't drinking at the moment – the names she's called Sadie in the past after she interviewed her. She said she was tricked into saying things she never meant, but we all know that was the alcohol.

'Hi, Mum,' I say as I step inside, trying to stay calm. 'Sadie's popped in to say hello.'

And she's also wondering if my brother or my husband is a serial killer.

The blood drains from my head. I feel as though the ground is about to swallow me.

Sadie grabs me by the elbow.

'Are you OK?' she says. 'Have you eaten yet this morning?'

I hold on to the radiator in the hall.

'I'll be fine,' I say, taking deep breaths and wiping the cold sweat from my brow. 'I just need a minute.'

I glance into the living room. Mum's sitting in her chair, smoking a cigarette.

'Mum,' I say, my voice weak. 'Why are you smoking in there?'

She stands, the cigarette still in her hand.

'Your phone's been going off,' she says, handing it to me. 'Someone called Liza's been calling and messaging. I didn't open it – I could tell from the screen.'

'Liza?' says Sadie as Mum returns to her chair. 'With a z? You don't hear that name often these days. Is that a friend?'

'Yes, yes,' I say distractedly. 'I met her about a year ago.'

'Liza Masters?'

'Masterson.' I peer into the bedroom. 'Mum!' I shout. 'Where's Mia?'

'Do you have a picture of this Liza?' says Sadie.

'Not now, Sadie.'

'Billy took Mia out,' says Mum. 'Mia said you promised her a milkshake.'

'What?'

'We didn't know how long you'd be, Jess.' She keeps looking at Sadie with narrowed eyes. 'Can I get either of you a drink?' She grinds her cigarette into the ashtray and stands. 'Long time no see, eh, Sadie?' she says. 'How's your sister?'

'Heather's OK,' says Sadie. 'Actually, she isn't. Our mother's recently had another heart attack. The doctor said she might have days, or she might have weeks.'

Mum's expression softens; she uncrosses her arms.

'I'm so sorry about that, Sadie.'

'That's good of you to say, Marie.'

Their gaze is locked. Sadie can't bear the sight of my mother.

'Mum gave up drinking six months ago,' I say quickly, inappropriately. 'You're doing really well, aren't you, Mum?'

'One day at a time,' she says, maintaining Sadie's gaze.

I want to part them with my hands, but it might make the situation volatile. You never know when Mum will snap. At least, for now, Sadie hasn't shared her theory with her. That she thinks my mum was lying when she said Billy was at home.

Which Sadie's probably wrong about. And, let's face it, she's not a trained detective; she's a journalist. The nose for a story is more important to her than getting justice. Or so it seemed, until now.

'Did Billy take Mia as soon as I left?' I ask, my mind going places I don't want it to go. I can feel Sadie's words, even though she hasn't said them out loud. 'Did he suggest it or did you?'

'Actually it was Mia,' says Mum. 'She mentioned the milk-shake. She needed a little persuading to go with him and not wait for you, but then Billy showed her a picture of him and her on his phone – he was holding her as a baby. He told her that he gave her Buggles – that teddy she said she always sleeps with.'

'Ah, OK.'

I daren't look at Sadie's expression. One single conversation with her and she has me distrusting my husband, my brother, my mother, for God's sake. How the hell has she managed that? I glance at my phone. I'll give it twenty minutes and if Billy and Mia aren't home, I'll go out looking for them.

It'll be fine. It'll be fine.

The tension is broken when Sadie's phone bleeps with a message.

'It's Heather,' she says, opening the front door. 'I need to go. Jessie, I'll give you a ring later. Bye, Marie.'

Mum closes the door.

'Well, well, well,' she says. 'What the fuck did that bitch want?'

CHAPTER 33
SADIE

17th April 2022

Sadie Harrison – Investigative Journalist

Liza Masters (LM)

Location: 16 Abbey Street, York.

Notes:

I hadn't seen Liza for almost ten years when she knocked on the door of my house yesterday. I almost didn't recognise her. Her hair was cut into a strange style that's short at the front and slightly longer at the back. She said she was in the area and that her mother had given her my address.

I am not totally convinced that Evelyn Masters has my home address.

SH: Here's your coffee, Liza. I hope it's not too strong.

LM: Do you tape every conversation you have?

SH: When it concerns a story – a case – that I'm working on.

LM: Right. You didn't used to tape my mum and me when we saw you last.

SH: Your mum didn't agree to being recorded.

LM: Who are those photos of on the wall?

(…)

LM: You didn't need to cover them. I'm not going to tell anyone.

SH: How's your mother doing?

LM: Not good. I think she forgets that she had two children, not just one. I don't blame her, really. Katie was the pretty one, she was the brainy one. She had everything. It's not fair that my mum lost her and was lumbered with me. *I'd* be annoyed if I were the one left.

SH: I'm sure that's not the case.

LM: So you've been talking to Rosie McShane?

SH: Why do you ask?

LM: The files over there have her name on it.

SH: Oh. I see. Yes.

LM: I've heard about that case. I looked it up online. She's had a daughter, hasn't she?

SH: How do you know that?

LM: I'm good on the internet. I'm on two of those sleuthing forums. I know how to get onto the Dark Web, as well.

SH: You said you had some information about your sister's case.

LM: Mum told me you used to talk to her. She was that one who was sent to Castleton Secure Unit. You said you didn't think Rosie McShane killed that girl, Lauren Jones. You thought the same person was killing other girls. Who do you think it is? Do you think it's one of those two men on your board? Do you think they killed my sister?

SH: You certainly know a lot about her case. That's something I'm working on.

LM: Ah, OK. I could find them for you if you want. Like I said…

SH: You're good at finding people. Are you OK, Liza?

LM: What do you mean? Course, I'm fine.

SH: Are you keeping busy?

LM: What's that supposed to mean?

SH: You seem agitated.

LM: If I could find the person who did it, then Mum will be OK again.

SH: Is she talking to anyone about what happened?

LM: A therapist, you mean. Nah. She prefers to just block it out. She's angry all the time. If I found out who did it, I'd make sure they never hurt anyone else again. Then Mum would find some peace. She might start to love me again.

SH: What?

LM: How many lives has he ruined? It's not just the girls he killed; it affected the lives of their families, their friends. Hundreds of people left in tatters because he got off on murdering vulnerable girls. He's a coward.

SH: Don't do anything silly, Liza.

LM: I wouldn't call it silly, Sadie. I'd call it justice.

CHAPTER 34

HEATHER

I keep looking at the clock, but time doesn't really mean anything at the moment. All I want is for Sadie to make it here for Mum. I don't want to be alone with her when she goes. I don't think my heart can take it. The last time I was with someone when they died was my Lauren. I'm not strong enough for this, I'm really not.

Mum's breathing is tremendously slow. It takes almost twenty seconds for each breath in, and each breath out. Sometimes there's longer than that in between and I think it's time, and then she takes a noisy, rattly breath.

'Are you OK, Heather?' It's Paddy at the door. His voice is a whisper. 'Do you want me to bring you anything? A brew?'

'I'm OK, thanks.'

'Your sister shouldn't be too long,' he says.

'I know. I just want her here. She'll never forgive herself if she's not here to say goodbye.'

Paddy turns to look along the corridor.

'Here she is now.' He holds the door open for Sadie. 'Let me know if you two need anything.'

'Thanks, Paddy,' says Sadie, breathless.

He closes the door softly.

'You smell of fresh air,' I say to her. 'It's nice.'

She takes off her jacket and pulls the other chair closer to me, next to Mum's bed.

'It's windy out there.'

'Did you get the information you need?'

'Let's not talk about that now.' She takes out her phone. 'Do you remember that song Mum and Dad used to dance to at Christmas after they'd had two too many sherries?'

'Oh yes,' I say, smiling at the memory as tears fill my eyes for the tenth time this morning. '"Only You," by The Platters.'

The music plays from Sadie's mobile, and I search Mum's face for a flicker of recognition – a smile, maybe. A tear. But there's nothing. I squeeze her hand; Sadie puts hers over the top and rests the side of her head on Mum's covers.

'I feel like we're keeping her here,' I say. 'That she doesn't want to leave us. She hasn't woken since yesterday. Do you think she'll wake up again?'

'I don't know,' says Sadie. 'The doctor said she might have weeks.'

'It doesn't feel like she does, though.'

'I know.'

'Shall I play another song?' Sadie asks.

Mum takes a long breath in.

The room is silent as we wait for her to breathe out.

But it doesn't come.

The silence fills my ears with static.

Even though we expected this, I don't want it to be true.

My mum. My precious, gentle mother.

I climb onto the bed next to her and weep onto her chest.

CHAPTER 35

JESSIE

It's been almost an hour since Billy took Mia to the café. Mum has been calling him every five minutes, but he isn't answering.

'What if she's hurt?' I say, gripping the windowsill, looking out.

'Your brother wouldn't hurt Mia,' says Mum, her voice unsteady. 'Mia's his own flesh and blood.'

'I wasn't suggesting he'd hurt her.' I turn to glance at her. 'I meant what if she's been run over or something. He doesn't know how to look after children. I bet he's never had to do it before.'

Mum lights up her fifth cigarette in twenty minutes.

'He told Mia he'd teach her how to make daisy chains – they're probably at the park. And he looked after you often enough,' she says. 'From when you were about five years old. He was very mature for an eight-year-old.'

'You left him in charge of me when he was that young?'

'It was different, then,' she says, flapping a hand. 'Everyone did it. It was really safe in...'

She doesn't finish her sentence. It wasn't safe. It still isn't safe for children. Where we grew up wasn't a nice neighbourhood where everyone looked out for each other. People slapping children who weren't even theirs; parents leaving their children to feed and fend for themselves.

We need to be vigilant. I should've been vigilant. I shouldn't have left Mia on her own with Mum and Billy. But my god. If I can't trust my own mother, who else can I trust?

'Yes,' I say. 'It'll be fine. No one would dare snatch her with Billy looking after her. He's taller than he used to be, isn't he?'

Mum looks at me, perplexed.

'What are you talking about?' she says. 'He's exactly the same height he's been since he was eighteen. Maybe a little thinner. Perhaps he's taken the breakup harder than he lets on. She probably finished things with him. He's no ambition, not really. Always likes to big himself up. He's never had much luck with ladies. I bet he gets lonely on those oil rigs, too. He's turned out to be a bit of a loner, hasn't he? Poor Billy. I had such high hopes for him.'

I turn around.

'Eh?' I say. 'You're always going on about how ambitious he is – how well he's doing for himself. He's the golden child.'

'Golden child...' Her face is stony. 'I'm not going to call him out about his failures when he's not here. Just like how I tell *him* how well *you're* doing – with your beautiful daughter, your famous art studio. He probably thinks *you're* the golden child. You were always treated better than he was as a kid.'

'I... I don't know what to say.' I smile wryly. 'And my studio isn't famous.'

'You don't have to say anything. At least what I say about you is true – your painting was in a Sunday magazine. That's famous to me. I've never had to lie about that.'

I turn to face the window again.

'Oh, thank God,' I say, spotting him at the end of the road. 'He's here.'

I open the front door, expecting my daughter to be next to him, holding his hand.

But she isn't.

'Where's Mia?'

My brother starts running towards me – his face is soaked with tears.

'I don't know, Jess,' he says, his voice breaking. 'I just popped to the toilet – the lady said she'd keep an eye on her. I didn't want her coming in the gents; it's disgusting in there. When I came out, she was gone.'

'What's going on?' Mum's standing at the front door. 'Where's Mia?'

'He's lost her, Mum,' I shriek. 'Billy's lost my little girl.'

Mum runs out the house, out the gate, and down to the end of the street.

'Where is she, Billy?' she screams. 'Where is she? How could you lose her? She's only little.' She holds her mobile phone to her ear. 'Police, please. My granddaughter's been taken.'

I almost collapse onto a side wall.

This can't be happening.

CHAPTER 36

JESSIE

I bring up Mark's contact details – ignoring the ten or so messages from Liza – but when I call him again it goes straight to voicemail.

'Mark,' I yell into the phone, my voice battling with the wind. 'Where the hell are you? Mia's been taken. You need to be here, now!'

Mum takes hold of me and we walk back towards the house.

'What are we going to do, Mum?' I say. 'Billy, what was the name of the café – did anyone see who took her?'

'It was busy,' he says. 'Loads of people in there were getting breakfast. I'm so sorry, Jessie. If anything happens to her, I'll never forgive myself.'

'What was the name of the café?' I say again, grabbing both his arms.

'Hopscotch,' says Mum. She points to the road ahead. 'It's on the high street on the left.'

I let go of my brother, breaking into a run. I'm running faster than I did when I was a kid.

If I'm fast enough, I'll catch her.

She's probably sitting there, waiting for me.

I'm coming for you, my love.

I glance behind me, Billy's not far behind. I can see from here that he's crying again. Anguish is written on his face.

I'm so angry with him right now, but adrenaline is taking over.

I'm nearly at the café; I almost run into the A-board before I burst through the door.

People are standing – huddling in groups.

'Have you seen a little girl?' I shout over the noise. 'She's this tall.' I put a hand to my waist. 'She was wearing a dress with polka dots on it. She's only little. She's never been to this café before.' Everyone's just staring at me. 'Anyone? Please help me!'

A woman in an apron approaches me.

'I own this place, love,' she says. 'My name's Cedella. We've been looking for her. Mia, isn't it?' She puts her arm around me.

'Do you have security cameras?' I ask. 'What about that one there?'

'That only covers the till.' She looks over my shoulder. 'You're the dad, yes?'

'No,' says Billy, bending over, breathless. 'Uncle. I'm her uncle. I was only gone a minute. I asked a lady' – he scans the small café – 'she's not here, now. I asked her to watch Mia while I nipped to the gents.' He looks at Cedella. 'Did you see her? Did you see me ask her?'

'We've been so busy,' she says. 'I'm so sorry.'

I release myself from her arm and run through the door labelled *toilets*. There is only one ladies cubicle and it's empty. The door to the gents is closed. I pound it with my fist.

'I won't be a minute,' says a man's voice.

'Have you got my daughter in there?' I yell.

'What?' The toilet flushes. 'No. No, it's just me.'

The door opens and an elderly man is standing there.

'Are you looking for that little girl?' he says.

'Have you seen her?'

He shakes his head.

'I'm sorry, love, I haven't.'

I whip the door to the café open; the room is silent.

'Did anyone see her leave?' I ask, more calmly this time.

There's a sea of shaking heads.

I want to collapse to the floor, but that won't help my daughter.

Outside, I scream her name.

But there's nowhere for her to hide.

Just rows of houses.

I run along the road, scanning parked cars for any sign of her, but there's none.

'I can't believe this, Jess,' says Billy, shadowing me. 'I will never forgive myself if anything happens. I won't.'

'I won't forgive you, either,' I shout. 'What the hell were you thinking, leaving her on her own? You don't give a shit about anyone but yourself!'

'I'm sorry, Jess,' he says. The tears are streaming down his face. I've never seen him so distraught. 'I'm really sorry. But it was busy, there'll be cameras. I saw one behind the counter.'

'It only covers the till,' I say. 'She might've been hiding and you left her on her own. How long did you look for her?'

'About half an hour.' He can't look me in the eye. 'I was only gone two minutes at the most.'

'It was two minutes too long,' I shout. I want to shake him by the shoulders. 'What are we going to do? We can't just leave her here.'

'She's not here,' says Billy. 'I checked everywhere. I had the whole place looking. Everyone was calling her name. Mum called the police. We have to be there to talk to them.'

Billy takes me by the hand and gently tugs me in the direction of Mum's house.

It's one of the hardest things I have ever done, but I follow him.

CHAPTER 37

Wednesday, 13th March 2024

Girl Snatched While Visiting Grandmother

Police and volunteers have been seen searching back gardens and sheds for four-year-old Mia Donovan.

Mia was reported missing today after being taken from Hopscotch café, close to her grandmother's home. Mia is described as wearing a light pink dress with large polka dots, and white trainers. Her long dark brown hair was in a ponytail when she was last seen at seven thirty this morning. Her mother, Jessie Donovan, 42, is distraught and appeals to whoever has taken her daughter: 'Please. If you're listening to this and you have Mia, please bring her back. I am nothing without her.'

In a statement issued by police, they said Mia was accompanied by her uncle at seven o'clock this morning to the café on the high street. She had been visiting the town in Greater Manchester since Monday afternoon.

Cedella Campbell, owner of the café said, 'All hell broke loose, at just after seven thirty this morning. I didn't know what was going on at first,' she said. 'Then this tall guy came up to me screaming. He said he'd left his niece sitting at the table near the door while he went to the toilet. I told him that I hadn't seen her, poor thing. I didn't notice her. I wish he hadn't sat her there. It's a pretty safe area but leaving a young kiddie on her own is just asking for trouble. I hope she's found soon. I'm praying for her poor mother.'

If you, or anyone you know, sees or has seen Mia Donovan, the police ask that you contact them immediately using 999.

For live updates on this story, follow our blog on www.manchesternewstoday.com.

CHAPTER 38

JESSIE

Mum's waiting for us on her front step, smoking another cigarette.

She stands when she sees us.

'Did you find Mia?' she shouts.

I shake my head. I can't bear to say it.

'Come on, you two.' Mum puts her arms around Billy and me and opens the front door. 'Let's wait for the police. They should be here soon.' Mum's phone buzzes. 'Look,' she says, 'they've got those new amber alerts. Everyone in the area should get this message. It's got to help. Everybody in the whole town will be on the lookout.'

I linger on the doorstep.

'You two go in,' I say. 'I'm not going inside until she comes home.'

I scan the street; I'm on high alert for every movement I see and sound that I hear.

I almost jump out of my skin when my phone beeps with a message.

The most recent one from Liza pops up on my screen.

> I'm almost there

Almost where?

I tap to open her message thread. There are so many unread.

'What the hell?'

> Still no answer from Mark. I'll try again later.

> I've just been to his workplace and he's not there. No one has seen him.

> I've been to your house. The police are there.

> Are you OK, Jessie? Are you getting your messages?

> I've managed to get an early morning coach to Manchester. Will message when I'm almost there.

> Almost there. I'll be there for you. I need to repay you for your kindness. I'll help in any way I can.

There for me for what? She doesn't know Mia is missing. She certainly won't have known what was going to happen at three in the morning when she caught the bus. What is she talking about?

> I'm at the bus station. Is it Clayton? I think that's where you said your mum lives.

> I'm here. I'm going to ask around to see if anyone knows where your mum lives.

What on earth was she thinking, travelling all the way to Manchester without me replying to her? And how does she know my mother's name in order to ask where she lives?

What was it Sadie said when I mentioned Liza?

Is her surname Masters?

I type *Liza Masters* into Safari.

I tap onto images, and there are five or so pictures of her, standing next to an older woman.

Oh my God.

She's Katie Masters's sister. The girl who was killed in 2003. She's standing next to Evelyn Masters, the mother she always talks about.

Katie is one of the girls Sadie believes is a victim of either my brother or my husband. And suddenly it all clicks into place. Now, all of the strange things she's ever said to me make sense.

She's known who I am from the very moment we met.

CHAPTER 39

JESSIE

The police are here at last. Almost twenty minutes after my mum called them. Despite my protests, they huddle us inside, even though my instincts are screaming at me to stay outside and keep looking for my daughter.

'Just for a few moments,' says the woman in the grey suit. 'Just so I can hear you properly out of the weather.'

My little Mia, out there in the wind and the rain. Was she wearing a coat? Did she have the waterproof one? What if she's freezing cold on her own? She doesn't know her way back.

'Have you got people looking for her on the streets?' I ask. 'She's not familiar with the area. She won't know how to get back here.'

'Yes, yes, of course,' she replies; she must be a detective. 'We've had people out looking since we received the call. We dispatched a team to the Hopscotch café, and a police helicopter has been launched to assist the search. My name's DI Jem King, and this is PC Steve Bracknell.' She stands in the middle of the living room until Mum gestures for her to sit. The police officer in uniform remains standing by the living-room door. 'You came into the station to see us yesterday. Is that right?'

'Yes. There have been posts about my daughter being missing, but she wasn't. She's been with me, constantly. Until today. Are you sure there are people out there looking for her?' I look to them both. 'I don't want to be just sitting here if no one's looking for her.'

'There are dozens or more officers searching for Mia,' says Jem. 'She's very much a priority.'

'Can you find out who's been posting those things?' Mum asks. 'Surely they've got to be connected.'

'We have a team working on it.' Jem spins to face me. 'Where is Mia's father? Is he out looking for her?'

'No. I mentioned it to the police officer yesterday. I haven't been able to get in contact with him. They said they'd do a welfare check on him at the house.'

'Where do you live?'

'Just outside Cheltenham.'

She stands.

'I won't be a sec.' She pulls out her phone and takes it outside. The window's open and I don't know if she realises we can hear her. 'DI Jem King, Greater Manchester Police following up on a welfare check for a Mr Mark Donovan of... Right... Shit... OK.'

She's ended her call, but she's lingering outside.

'Mum?' I say, my heart rate rising again. 'What's going on?'

Mum's getting a cigarette out the packet. She stands and joins the detective outside. I hear the click of her lighter. Why aren't my legs allowing me to stand? It's like they're glued to the floor. They're protecting me from something I don't want to know.

'Jessie?' The detective appears next to me. 'I'm afraid I have some terrible news.'

'Oh, God,' I say. 'Have they found Mia? Oh God, please say she's not dead.'

'No, it's not about Mia.' She crouches down beside me. 'I'm afraid it's your husband, Mark. I'm so sorry to have to tell you this, but he's been found dead in your home. It looks as though he's been there for several days. I'm so sorry.'

I stand, the adrenaline giving my body a surge of energy.

'No.' I march outside to Mum. 'That's not right. Mum. They're saying Mark's dead but they must have the wrong person.'

'I don't think they have, love.' She puts her arms around me. 'I'm so sorry, Jessie. I'm so sorry.'

I put my arms around her.

'I can't do this, Mum,' I say. 'Why is this happening to me? Have I not been through enough? Why, Mum? Where's Mia? Where's Mark? They can't have both left me. It's not fair, Mum.'

She's stroking my hair.

'I know it's not, love. I know. It's just... it's awful. I'm so sorry, Jessie. We'll find Mia. We have to. The police will find her. They have everyone looking.'

I nod because I can't get any words out.

I just want to scream into the air, rewind the past three days and go back to the way things were.

My knees begin to wobble. I don't think I can stand any more.

As they buckle, my mother catches me.

'You can do this, Jessie,' she says. 'You can do this.'

'I don't think I'm strong enough any more,' I say. 'I really don't.'

CHAPTER 40

JESSIE

I'm sitting next to the window, blankly staring out because my life is falling to pieces. Liza must've known about Mark. That's why she's coming up. That's why she's been messaging and phoning me. If I had answered her call she might have given me a hint as to what has happened. She might've been the one who found him.

If I had spoken to her, I wouldn't have let Mia out of my sight.

Mia wouldn't be missing.

Why didn't I answer her calls?

Because I saw her as a nuisance. Someone I couldn't be bothered talking to.

Oh God. This is all such a mess.

What am I going to do?

My husband is dead.

Mark is dead.

It's not real. I can't process any of it when my beautiful daughter isn't here.

The detective is in the kitchen, talking to my mum as she makes us all a hot drink.

I turn to look at the officer standing at the door, and his gaze quickly shifts when I make eye contact.

He knows who I am, doesn't he?

I know it's meant to be confidential, but Nicola Parry would've been in contact with the lead detective. There's no way Jem King would have kept it to herself. And PC Steve Bracknell knows. I can see it in his eyes.

He probably thinks I deserve all of this.

That a child murderer shouldn't be allowed to have children of her own. Especially a daughter.

I turn to face the window again.

I don't care what he thinks. I don't care what anyone thinks.

DI Jem King pulled me aside a few moments ago to tell me that, usually, the parents take part in a televised appeal, but Nicola Parry thought it best if we issue a statement in case someone recognises me.

As Jem King walks back into the living room, I turn to face her.

'I'll do the appeal,' I say. 'I don't care if anyone recognises me.'

She frowns.

'It's not just for you, though, Jessie,' she says earnestly. 'It's so Mia is protected, too.'

Her sentiment gives me hope.

Protecting Mia from being identified as a McShane means there's some hope that Mia will be found alive.

It's what I need to cling onto.

'OK,' I say, returning to my position near the window. 'OK.'

'Hold on, Mia,' I say quietly. 'You'll be home soon, my lovely little girl.'

I grip my hands together in some sort of prayer. I close my eyes.

Please God. If you're really there. Please make sure my daughter comes back safely.

* * *

It's been three hours since my daughter went missing. The detective left an hour ago, and the uniformed police officer is guarding the door.

Billy's lying down in the spare bedroom – in the bed that Mia was in this morning when I stupidly left the house without her. I can hear him crying.

'This is ridiculous,' says Mum, standing up. 'Who does he think he is, sniffling like this when all of this is his fault in the first place?'

She opens the bedroom door.

'Come on, Billy,' she says. 'That's enough. You've got to come out and support your sister.'

'I can't bear to look at her, Mum,' he says, not realising I can hear every word. 'It's my fault. I wouldn't be able to live with myself if anything bad happened to Mia.'

'Stop feeling sorry for yourself.'

I stand and walk quietly into the hall, standing at the hinge of the door. He's sitting with his knees to his chest, rocking back and forth.

'I didn't mean to lose her, Mum,' he says. 'Honestly, I didn't.'

'It wasn't one of your dodgy friends, was it?' says Mum. 'You said last week you had some gambling debts with some scary people. Would one of them have done this?'

What the hell is she talking about?

'No. I haven't got any dodgy friends. And the debt's been paid off,' he says. 'I only knew one scary person and now he's dead.'

'Well, it can't have been him, can it?'

'Jessie shouldn't have married him. He shouldn't have been allowed to have a daughter.'

'What are you talking about?'

'I needed money, Mum. I thought he'd lend it to me, but he didn't. I kept quiet about how he was with little girls. He couldn't be trusted around them.'

'Are you making things up again, Billy?'

'What do you mean?'

'Like when you weren't where you said you were. When Lauren—'

'Mum, please don't do this now.'

'Did you have anything to do with it?' she asks him.

'Of course I didn't. You have to believe me. Please, Mum.'

'I don't have to believe you,' she says, leaning closer to him. 'I lied for you all those years ago because I thought I had to protect you. Told the police you were at home, but you'd only just run inside. And then it turned out that I had to say those words in court, even though it would implicate my very own daughter.'

I audibly gasp.

My knees can't support me. I collapse onto the floor.

This is what Sadie's been hinting at for years. She as good as told me this morning.

Why didn't she just blurt it out and say it?

I can't believe I'm finding out like this.

If I hadn't been standing by the door, I wouldn't have known at all.

I want to sink into the floor; I want to disappear.

I want to be wherever my daughter is and never see these people again.

These two people. The only family I have right now.

And they betrayed me in the worst possible way.

'Oh God, Jessie,' says Mum, tearing out the room. 'Please tell me you didn't hear any of that? Please, Jessie.'

I stagger to the front door. There are already reporters standing outside.

'Jessie,' says Mum. 'Please don't go out there – it won't be safe for you if they take your picture. Please. Think of Mia.'

'How could you, Mum? How could you lie for him, when it was me who was on trial for her murder?'

'I didn't think he had anything to do with it, did I? He would've gone to prison for twenty years. I didn't know, when they first came to the door, that Heather had seen you. Really, I didn't. If I could take it back, I would. I'm so sorry, Jessie.'

'You have to tell the police.'

Billy opens the bedroom door. He stands, looming over me.

'Jessie, don't tell the police,' he says. 'What does it matter now?'

'You're sick,' I say, shoving him back into the room. 'What about all those other girls: Lila, Katie... They were just kids. Why would you do that to them?'

'I've no idea what you're talking about.'

'What have you done to Mia? Where did you put her?' I start pounding his chest with my fists. 'Tell me, Billy. For God's sake, tell me where she is.'

I collapse onto the floor.

The police officer is standing in the hall.

'Is everything all right, Mrs Donovan?'

I glance up at him to see that his bodycam light is on.

'How much of that did you hear?'

'Enough,' he says. 'Detective King is on her way back.'

Billy steps over me, pushes past me and Mum. The police officer's head comes to my brother's shoulders and offers barely any resistance to my brother as he exits the room.

'Wait,' says the officer. 'Billy McShane, I advise you not to leave this house.'

He chases after him as Billy exits the house. I cover my head as I leave the house, but none of the reporters take my photograph.

'Jessie!' I turn around to see Liza, walking towards me. 'I'm so sorry about Mark. His mum went round to your house at the same time I did. She... she found him: Mark. He was in the kitchen. There looked like there'd been a struggle. God, it was so horrible.'

'Liza, Mia's missing,' I say, the words alien to me. I can't think of my husband right now – my mind can't take it. 'She's been missing since this morning. The police are looking for her. I don't know what to do.'

'Shall we go inside?'

'I don't know.' I cling to her arm, even though she's almost a stranger. She's been lying about who she is for months. 'What am I going to do, Liza?'

'She'll be fine,' she says pensively. 'We have to believe that. The world wouldn't be so cruel as to take her away from you. Not after all that you've been through.'

'What do you mean?'

'It's OK, Jessie,' she says, putting her arm tightly around me. 'You don't have to pretend with me.'

CHAPTER 41

HEATHER

'I don't want to leave her, Sadie,' I say. 'Shall we go back inside? They said we could stay as long as we wanted.'

We're sitting in Sadie's car, still in the grounds of The Haven. We sat with Mum for three hours. I brushed her hair. We played the music that she liked. We opened the patio door to let in the fresh air and a beautiful white butterfly fluttered inside.

'There'll still be time to visit Mum,' says Sadie. 'We'll have to pick out an outfit for her.'

'We don't have to do that today, though?'

'No. Not today.' She puts the keys in the ignition. 'Shall we head back to yours? Are you ready?'

'I suppose.'

We travel with the windows open, no music. The gusts of wind blow through my hair, reminding me that I'm still alive. The one left behind.

Sadie reaches over and taps my knee.

'You've still got me, remember,' she says. 'And Eddie. You can't forget Eddie.'

'No,' I say with a smile. 'There's no forgetting Eddie.'

We pull up outside and the house looks exactly the same. I don't know why I expected it to look any different. Perhaps we will move, after all. There's a shadow over the place that I've not noticed before.

'Eddie, we're home,' I yell, as I unlock the front door. 'Where are you, Eddie?'

He appears at the kitchen door, blocking the entrance.

'You're gonna go mad at me,' he says. 'It was a spur of the moment thing. I followed a man who took Mia out of Marie McShane's house. It was the same man I saw watching the house last night. At first, I thought he was taking her to see her mum, Rosie. You were with Rosie, weren't you, Sadie? And then he went in the opposite direction. It looked like he sneaked her out the house. I panicked. I worried that he might harm her.'

'What on earth are you going on about, Eddie?'

He stands aside.

There's a little girl sitting at the kitchen table, swinging her legs as she colours people's faces in magazines with a blue biro.

She looks up at me and smiles.

'Have you brought my mummy?' she says. 'She's taking a long time hide-and-seeking me.'

Sadie nudges me gently aside.

'Eddie,' she says, 'you took Mia Donovan? What the hell were you thinking?'

* * *

Eddie stays in the car as Sadie and I help Mia out.

Marie McShane's door flies open, and Rosie – Jessie – dashes down the path, taking her little girl into her arms.

'Oh, Mia, my baby,' she says. 'I was so worried about you. Are you OK? Did Eddie hurt you?'

She pats her little girl down, checking for cuts or bruises.

'I'm OK, Mummy,' says Mia. 'I was waiting for you.'

'You shouldn't have gone with that man,' Jessie scolds. 'You were supposed to stay with Uncle Billy.'

'I didn't like Uncle Billy,' says Mia. 'He kept telling me to hold his hand when I didn't want to. He sat me on the seat and said, *Stay there!* His nails were all dirty and yucky.'

'Come on, honey,' says Jessie. 'Let's get you inside.' She glances over her shoulder. 'Tell Eddie to wait in the car. The detective is on her way.'

The venom in her voice is understandable. I feel terrible about this whole thing. It's just so out of control. What the devil was my husband thinking? He's ruined everything.

A woman goes to close Marie McShane's door. It must be one of Rosie's friends.

'Liza?' Sadie takes a step forward. 'Liza Masters? What are you doing here?'

The door slams shut.

CHAPTER 42

JESSIE

I don't want to let my daughter go. I'm clinging to her tightly and she's getting slightly annoyed with me. It's hard to smile after the past few hours, but I can't help myself.

Sadie's sitting in Mum's chair, still in her coat.

'I'm so sorry again, Jessie,' she says. 'I had no idea Eddie was going to take her. It's totally out of character for him. He's been going through a lot. I've only recently told him that Lauren's...' She glances at Mia. 'That her case hasn't been solved. That police got the wrong person. He thought he was protecting Mia. He saw you and I leave the house and he thought your brother was snatching Mia.'

'You don't have to keep explaining,' I say. 'I'm not saying I agree with him taking her, but I understand. If only he'd have taken her straight to the police station if he thought she was in danger.'

'He wasn't thinking straight,' she says. 'I'm so sorry, Jessie.'

'Mummy,' says Mia. 'Will that man get into trouble?'

'I hope so,' I say, glancing at Liza who's standing at the kitchen door.

'But he said he was protecting Mia,' says Liza. 'You don't

want to see him in prison after all that he's been through, surely?'

'It's not up to me,' I say. 'It's up to the police. You can't just go round taking children off the street. What message will that send out?'

'I know,' says Liza. 'It's just that it seems unfair, that's all.'

'Life's not fair sometimes.' I try to keep the bitterness out of my voice. 'If they had kept looking for Lauren's...' I censor myself in front of Mia. 'Then he might not have gone on to do other things.' I look at Liza. 'Why didn't you tell me who you were?'

She sits next to me on the settee. I shuffle away slightly.

'I didn't want you to think I was some kind of stalker.'

'It's creepy, Liza. Don't you understand that?'

I shouldn't be saying such cruel things to her; her sister was murdered. She's had to grow up without her – a shadow cast over her family. It's like the cloud that hangs over mine; a thunderous presence that's been here since I was a child.

'I'm sorry, Jessie,' she says. 'Will you ever forgive me?'

'I can't think about it right now.' My mind flashes to Mark. 'It doesn't seem real that he's gone...'

'Is Marie still in the toilet?' says Mia, unaware of what I'm talking about. 'When can we go home?'

'Soon, love,' I say. 'We're waiting for that nice police detective to come round. She says she has something she wants to show us.'

I need to go to talk to Mum but I don't feel safe leaving Mia anywhere – even in this house.

'Let's go and see if Marie's OK, shall we, Mia?' I lead her to the bathroom door.

'I can watch her,' Sadie offers. 'She'll be OK, won't you, Mia? I've not much experience of looking after children, so you'll have to look after me. Is that all right?'

Mia nods. 'I will. I can do that. And I don't need to go to the bathroom, Mummy,' she says. 'But when I do, I don't want you coming in with me again. I'm big, now.'

'I know you are, Mia,' I say. 'Just for a little while. I need to make sure you're with me all the time.'

I tap on the door.

'Mum. Are you OK in there?'

She opens the door.

'I'm going to tell them everything,' she says. Her face is blotchy, red, damp. 'Everything that I know about that day, about Billy. It's my fault that Mia went missing today.'

'Why is it your fault?' asks Liza, tilting her head to the side.

I know Liza's trying to stick up for me, but she doesn't know my mother. I try to shrug off the uneasiness of her standing next to me when I'm trying to confront my mother. But it's not as though I can ask her to leave. Her sister was one of my brother's victims, for goodness' sake.

'If Jessie hadn't been...' Mum starts. 'If Billy...' She looks at Liza. 'I'm so sorry about your sister – about Katie.' She looks to the ceiling. 'God, what a time to stop drinking.'

'Do what you feel is right, Mum,' I say. 'Everything will be OK.'

I know what will happen, though. I shouldn't be saying that to her. The police will charge her with perverting the course of justice, at the very minimum.

Mum knows this, too.

This is our long goodbye.

A car pulls up outside and I open the door to let Detective King, and a man I don't recognise, inside.

'This is Detective Inspector Trevor Bennett. He's from Gloucestershire Constabulary.' She lowers her voice. 'He's on the investigation team looking into your husband's death.'

'Shall I take Mia into the bedroom?' asks Sadie.

'OK,' I say hesitantly. 'Make sure the window's locked.'

I've told Mia that her daddy has died, but I don't think she's taken it in. Everything's happened so quickly and she's been through so much that it might take days, weeks, for the realisation to sink in. My poor little girl.

Jem King and Trevor Bennett file into the living room. She places a laptop on my mum's small smoking table.

'The camera facing your back garden was smashed,' says King, opening the computer and signing in, 'but the ones near the front door and at the side of your house were working.'

She clicks the *play* icon on the screen and it plays a montage of my husband returning from the train station on the morning Mia and I left for Manchester. Three hours later, a man in a baseball cap approaches the front door, peak down. He must have known the camera was there.

'Do you recognise this man?' DI King asks.

'No,' I say. 'Not from just the hat.'

'Hang on,' she says. 'I'll fast forward until... What about now?'

'Yes.' I lean closer. 'That's my brother. He was wearing that baseball jacket when he came here. You don't think he has anything to do with it, do you?'

'Also,' she says. 'Do you recognise this woman?'

She plays the footage of Liza, standing outside my house.

'Yes,' I say. 'She was on the phone to me at the time. She said she saw someone inside the house hiding from her. I asked her to go round because I hadn't heard from Mark.'

'OK,' she says. 'That fits with what Liza said to Gloucestershire police. We'll of course obtain phone records to double check the times.'

'I know you've been through a lot, Jessie,' says Trevor Bennett, speaking for the first time. 'But we have reasons to believe it was your brother posting false missing reports about your daughter on social media. There was a transaction from your husband's business account to your brother's personal account on Monday, the eleventh of March, at four in the afternoon.

'We believe he was blackmailing your husband. Has anything happened between the two of them in the past? Something that one knows about the other?'

'There could be a whole host of things,' I say. 'Sadie Harrison – she's a journalist. She's interviewed a lot of people about Mark and Billy. You should talk to her.'

Jem King closes the laptop; they both stand.

'Are you heading back to Gloucestershire?' she asks.

'Yes,' I say. 'Today, I think. Sadie and Liza are going to travel with me. I've nothing keeping me here any more.' I'm looking at my mother as I say that final sentence.

'I'd better come with you,' Mum says to the two police officers. 'I can't tell you here. Not in front of my daughter, and not in the same house as my granddaughter.'

'Um, OK,' says King, visibly confused. 'See you, Jessie. Either Trevor or I will give you a ring when we have further news. Have a safe trip back. I'm so sorry about your husband.' She opens the spare bedroom door, where Sadie's looking over Mia's shoulder as she plays a game on my phone. 'Bye, bye, Mia. It was lovely to meet you.'

'Bye, Jem,' she says, looking up.

'I think she's going to be OK,' King says to me before heading out the door. 'In time.'

'I hope you're right.'

'Come on, ladies,' I say, affecting a cheerful tone that doesn't match my mood. 'Let's get packing. I don't want to be in this house a moment longer than I have to.'

CHAPTER 43

JESSIE

We've been staying at this Airbnb for almost two weeks. Mia's school doesn't go back until the fifteenth of April, which is a good thing because she keeps waking in the night asking for her daddy. And each time I tell her, it's like the first time she's hearing it. It breaks my heart every time.

I still haven't decided whether or not she should come to his funeral, but I need to decide soon because it's the day after tomorrow.

Sadie's bicycle bell dings as she comes up the drive. She's been amazing these past two weeks. She drove us back to Cheltenham and helped us find this place to stay. After her mother's funeral, she returned to help us get through Mark's; she's staying in a lovely B&B by the river with her sister, Heather.

I've barely heard from Liza, but I'm not surprised. She found me to get close to the person she thought killed her sister. I shudder every time I think about it, though I know I shouldn't be afraid of her.

I'm so glad Sadie's been around for Mia and me, though. Even though she's mourning the loss of her mother. These past few weeks have been some of the worst I've ever had. But I know I can get through it. As long as I have my daughter with me, I can get through anything.

I flick on the kettle before I open the door for her.

'Thanks so much for this,' I say, leading her into the kitchen. 'Are you sure you don't mind taking her out? I shouldn't be too long.'

She takes off her helmet and places it on the side.

'I don't mind at all,' she says. 'It'll be fun. Is Mia doing OK? How many times did she wake last night?'

'Just once.'

'Well, that's progress.'

'Help yourself to a tea or coffee,' I say. 'You know where everything is. I'll just go and see if she's awake yet.'

* * *

I'm sitting on Mia's bed, willing her to wake because it's almost eleven o'clock and she was so excited about getting a milkshake before she went to sleep last night.

It's like she can read my mind; she opens her eyes and turns to face me.

'I knew you were there, Mummy,' she says. 'Were you there all night because I could feel you at the end of the bed?'

A shiver runs through me, but I dismiss any spooky thoughts.

'It must've been Squishy,' I say, picking up her new giant teddy that's fallen to the floor.

'It's milkshake and ice cream and burger day,' she says, sitting up and getting out of bed.

'Who added the ice cream and burger?' I ask, smiling.

'I added the ice cream, and Sadie added the burger when she came round last night.'

'I should've guessed.'

She opens one of her drawers and takes out her new jeans and her new bright yellow jumper.

'I dreamed Daddy was an angel,' she says. 'And he says he's OK.'

'That's nice, love.'

'And he said that I could have two milkshakes if I needed them.'

'Really?' I say, keeping my lips straight. 'That's very kind of him to say.'

'I know. I'm gonna try the strawberry and the chocolate.'

'Very, well, Miss Donovan. Two milkshakes it is. I'll give Sadie a list.'

'Thank you, Mummy. And if I can't finish them, I can take them home and remember Daddy with them.'

'That's a lovely idea, Mia.'

'It wasn't my idea, silly.'

She takes me by the hand and pulls me out the room and down the stairs.

'Sadie,' she shouts. 'It's café time.'

'I'm ready,' says Sadie. 'Especially as you're paying, Mia.'

I grab the large canvas and place it in the boot of the car.

Sadie clicks in Mia's seatbelt.

'We can walk back if you want to take longer,' she says, getting into the back seat next to Mia – she's getting to be as protective as I am. 'Are you sure you're going to be OK?'

'I'll be fine.'

I belt up and start the car. Mia chats the whole way to the little café on the corner. I watch as Sadie holds her by the hand as they order from the counter. I linger long enough to realise that she's going to be OK with Sadie. It helps that I'm tracking the tag I sewed into Mia's little jacket. You can never be too careful.

* * *

It's only a short drive to the bed and breakfast. It's a pretty place that overlooks the river. She's waiting for me in the small bar area. She stands as I walk in and looks as nervous as I feel.

'Hello, Heather,' I say.

We're not at the hugging stage just yet, though.

'Hello, Jessie,' she says. 'What have you got there?'

I hand her the canvas and she places it on the table as we sit.

'It's for you,' I say, trapping my nervous hands under my legs. 'I've spent years working on it.'

She carefully removes the string, and peels off the brown paper, to reveal my painting of Lauren. In it, she's wearing her Walkman headphones, listening to Take That. Her hair's been lightened by the sun; freckles are dotted on her nose. The loveliest, most caring best friend a little girl could ask for. We were always together and, whenever I close my eyes, she's still next to me.

'Oh, Jessie,' says Heather. 'It's just beautiful. It's like looking at a photo, but you've captured her essence, her sunshine. Thank you so much.'

She reaches into her leather handbag and takes out a photograph.

'It was when you went to the beach.' She hands it to me. 'The summer before you started high school. Do you remember?'

'Of course I remember.'

I look down at us. Heads close together, each of us with an ice cream held up to our mouths. The light and joy in our eyes, our giant smiles; our hair plastered across our faces.

This is how I will always remember us.

EPILOGUE

Billy McShane Jailed For Life
By Sadie Harrison

William 'Billy' McShane, 48, of Clayton, Manchester, has today been handed five life sentences for the murders of Lauren Jones, Lila Foster, Paige Lewis, Katie Masters, and Mark Donovan.

McShane had denied being responsible for the killings, but a jury found him guilty after deliberating for only five hours following a two-month trial where it was revealed Billy McShane's DNA was found at three of the five crime scenes.

The verdict and sentencing come after his sister Rosie McShane was given a full pardon after being wrongfully convicted of the murder of her friend Lauren Jones in 1994. Rosie was awarded an undisclosed sum in compensation for her wrongful conviction. Her mother, Marie McShane, admitted that the alibi she gave her son Billy McShane in March of 1994 was false. She has since been sentenced to four years in prison.

The families of Katie, Lila, and Paige have expressed their relief that their daughters have finally got the justice they deserved. Liza Masters, who lives just outside Cheltenham, said, 'I have always sought justice for my sister, Katie. I've had to grow up without my big sister. My mother's life was ruined by what happened to her daughter. Billy and his friend have been in my sights for a long time. I want to say a sincere thank you to the police. This has been a long and painful journey for everyone involved.'

A LETTER FROM ELISABETH CARPENTER

Dear Reader,

I want to say a huge thank you for choosing to read *The Girl on the News*. I hope you enjoyed it and, if you did, I would be very grateful if you could write a review. I'd love to hear what you think, and it makes such a difference helping new readers to discover one of my books for the first time.

I love hearing from my readers – you can get in touch with me through social media or my website.

If you want to keep up to date with all my latest releases, just sign up at the following link. Your email address will never be shared and you can unsubscribe at any time.

www.bookouture.com/elisabeth-carpenter

Very best wishes,

Elisabeth

facebook.com/ElisabethCarpenterAuthor

x.com/LibbyCPT

ACKNOWLEDGEMENTS

Thank you to my agent, Caroline Hardman. Thank you to the team at Hardman & Swainson. Huge thanks to my wonderful, amazing editor Susannah Hamilton, whose notes and suggestions have been invaluable in making this book what it is. Thank you also to the fantastic team at Bookouture. Thank you to my friends and family; your unwavering support keeps me going.

Thank you to my wonderful readers – I hope you enjoy this one!

PUBLISHING TEAM

Turning a manuscript into a book requires the efforts of many people. The publishing team at Bookouture would like to acknowledge everyone who contributed to this publication.

Audio
Alba Proko
Sinead O'Connor
Melissa Tran

Commercial
Lauren Morrissette
Jil Thielen
Imogen Allport

Cover design
Jules Macadam

Data and analysis
Mark Alder
Mohamed Bussuri

Editorial
Susannah Hamilton
Nadia Michael

Made in United States
Orlando, FL
05 February 2024

43337047R00168